Holly for Christmas:
A Holiday Romantic Novella

CHERYL BARTON

Published by:
Barton Publishing, LLC

This book is a work of fiction. Any references or similarities to actual events, real people, living or dead, or to real places, are intended to give the novel a sense of reality. Any similarities in names, characters, places and incidents is entirely coincidental.

Barton Publishing, LLC
P.O. Box 962
Reisterstown, Maryland 21136
www.crbarton.com

Ordering Information:
Quantity sales. Special discounts are available on quantity purchases by corporations, associations, and others. For details, contact the publisher at the address above.

Orders by U.S. trade bookstores and wholesalers. Please contact prez@crbarton.com

ISBN: 0615944744
ISBN-13: 978-0615944746

Dear Reader,

It's Christmas time and I thought I'd release a short story to spread some holiday cheer.

For a man who hates holidays, Timothy Cornish's bah humbug heart is melted when he meets Holly Day.

I hope you enjoy *Holly For Christmas*.

Happy Reading!

Thank you,
Cheryl Barton

ACKNOWLEDGMENT

Shout out to the greatest family, friends and fans found anywhere!

I am an author because of you.

1

Bah humbug!

Timothy Cornish didn't just feel this way because it was the Christmas season, he felt this way all year round, every day of the week, but most of all, he hated Christmas. It was a holiday that never meant anything to him. He had no family to celebrate with like most people may have and though he had great friendships, he found himself jealous of the time they spent with family around the holidays, especially this time of year. For him, it was best to avoid people around any day that would bring about a celebration like his birthday, Thanksgiving and Christmas and pretty much any day that would require a store to put out greeting cards.

Growing up in group homes and floating around in the foster care system, all of the days blended together and though some of those places had some semblance of celebrating a holiday, it wasn't the big production he'd hear other kids with families brag about. The one thing he remembered most that he wanted and wished for was a family to call his own, but he was never adopted by one. He remained in the foster care system until he aged out.

Whoever his parents were, they'd left him on the steps of a catholic church in New York City not long after his birth. To this day, he had no family to speak of and after the hard life he'd lived as a child, he didn't have a desire to look for them. He was still too angry and bitter feeling like he wasn't wanted by anyone. Even if he did want to look, he wouldn't know where to start. The only information found with him in the basket that he was found in was a note saying he was two months old and what day he had been born.

After being discovered on a cold, snowy night the day before Christmas, he was turned over to child services. He was given his name by the court after a worker at child services recommended a name. The worker loved the name Timothy Cornish after reading it in one of her favorite novels. She loved the strong male character and hoped for the same for the cute little boy left without a family. The court agreed when no one came forward to claim him or could claim they knew who his parents were. They tried checking fingerprint and footprint records and came up empty. Timothy had later been told that they believed whoever gave birth to him, probably did so at home without any type of medical care.

From the age of two months until age eighteen, he bounced around, never feeling wanted, something no child should ever endure.

He watched from year to year as children came and went from the group homes and foster homes he'd lived in, getting adopted by families while he stayed feeling unloved and unwanted.

Timothy's childhood had been one disappointment after

another and holidays were the worst. He was sick and tired of everyone walking around wishing him a Happy Thanksgiving or a wonderful Easter and of course the worst being well-wishers at Christmas-time. He hated it and he never returned the sentiment, causing people to sneer at him. If someone wished him something happy, he simply grunted back his response and his immediate mood was, Bah humbug!

When he turned eighteen and could no longer stay at any group homes and families no longer received money for his care in the foster care system, he was left to take care of himself. Luckily, he was smart enough to get good grades in school and because of his situation, he was able to get money that covered the years he'd attended college. He'd had odd jobs for years and was frugal with his money knowing he only had himself to rely on for survival.

While in college in New York, he rented a room from a nice family right near the school, worked several jobs and proudly graduated with a degree in business management. After graduation, he realized he had a knack for selling and started working at a local real estate company. It didn't take him long to excel in his field of work, becoming one of the company's million dollar sellers, time and time again.

One day when he had enough money to finally leave New York, which brought him nothing but bad memories, he relocated to Chicago. After a few years of successful home sales in a market prime for new real estate, he was able to start his own real estate company, TRC Realty and things continued to look up for him. He was successful at work and was proud of how his life turned out considering where he started, but still something was missing. He was happy professionally, but personally, his life pretty much sucked.

He was able to maintain a full staff of employees who all seemed to like their job working for him. Though he knew he wasn't the easiest person to work for and there were days he knew they made sure they avoided running into him, he paid them well and business seemed to always be booming even with the downturn the economy had taken that impacted the real estate business. Even in the midst of that, he used his experience and education in business management and learned how to maintain in the sluggish economy. When he succeeded, his staff succeeded, so the good outweighed even his tyrant ways.

Now that Thanksgiving had finally passed, his mood had picked up a little. He had friends who'd invited him over for every holiday because they knew he had no family to speak of. Sometimes he accepted, but not this year. He wanted to spend Thanksgiving relaxing at home to avoid large groups of people who would be singing, drinking and having a good time. There was a time when his employees would invite him over as well and when he never accepted, they finally stopped inviting. He knew he needed to improve his mood, but his past wouldn't let him enjoy his future when it came to celebrations.

He wasn't the friendliest person and he wasn't sure he knew how to be overly friendly like he saw in others. Following him around day after day was the persona that he didn't like people, hated holidays and disliked even more, people who loved holidays.

Bah humbug!

Timothy tried not to keep his staff from celebrating the holidays, especially around the office. He allowed them to decorate for every holiday and have office parties,

4

something he never took time to take part in and made excuses for other obligations he needed to meet so that he didn't have to stick around. Thomas figured he did his part by contributing the bulk of the expense for any decorating or celebrations. They appreciated it, but he could see their disappointment when it was time for his next excuse to vacate all activities.

At thirty-seven, Timothy had wealth in material things that should make anyone happy to be in his shoes. He lived in a large house in an affluent section of Chicago and several times, he'd been approached about having his home featured in one magazine or another, a request he always turned down. He owned several expensive cars and when he felt like it, he sometimes attended the most popular parties in town and entertained the wealthiest in the Chicago area. All of that meant nothing whenever he had another achievement and he had no one that he could call to celebrate with. He had friends, but it wasn't the same as if he'd had a family.

Timothy wasn't sure what he was missing because he'd never had it. This was his life, day in and day out and again, the cause for his mantra of bah humbug! Perhaps, today would have been a good day to work from home, he thought as he walked into this office, clearly in a non-festive mood.

"Good morning Mr. Cornish. Here are some messages for you that I retrieved from the messaging service that came in after hours yesterday. Would you like your usual cup of coffee this morning?" his office assistant Ariana asked as he entered.

His mind was so preoccupied with where he'd come from, he wasn't focused on where he was going and almost walked right by his assistant. He stopped and smiled.

"Good morning, Ariana. Thank you for the messages," he said taking them from her and quickly scrolled through them while heading into his own office.

"Coffee Mr. Cornish?" she hollered after him.

His mind was still preoccupied.

"Don't worry about the coffee. I had a cup at home this morning. Is Jeffrey in yet?" he inquired.

"Yes, would you like for me to have him step into your office?"

"Tell him I'd like to get together with him as soon as he gets a free moment."

Jeffrey was one of the greatest assets to his team of realtors. There were new clients that needed help and he knew Jeffrey would be the perfect person to get on it. His own time would be taken up by one particular client who only wanted to work with him. He didn't usually take that type of a request, but after receiving information about what the client needed, he decided to handle this one himself, so he would hand over the control of other clients to Jeffrey in order to free up his own schedule.

When the request first came in, he shifted it to someone else, which was unlike him for a client with such a high dollar value. He saw the words children's home and bad memories surfaced and his initial response was to stay away because he wanted no parts of it. One day after leaving the office, he couldn't shake the feeling that he should be the one to help the client and decided he would, in fact, take on this one himself. Something about it drew him in where he initially wanted to back away. He would have his Ariana call the client later in the day and schedule a meeting to go over specifics of what they were looking for. For now, he had other calls to make and a few new clients to assign to his staff.

"Mr. Cornish?" Aria called over the intercom.

"Yes, Ariana," he responded.

"Mr. Walsh is on line two for you."

"Thank you," he said, grabbing his phone to connect with his best friend, Kenneth Walsh.

"What's up Ken? To what do I owe this early morning phone call from you?"

"Cynthia and I were concerned when the weekend passed and we didn't hear from you. You know we wanted you over for Thanksgiving and hoped you'd grace us with your presence this year. You know little Kenny has asked about you several times. Of course, he loves beating his uncle Timothy in video games."

Cynthia and Kenneth had been married for seven years and were the closet to family he had, especially since he didn't have any real family.

Kenneth was his best friend and had actually sold him his first car when he lived in New York. Years ago, Kenneth packed up and moved is family to Chicago and through conversations about opportunities, he made the decision to relocate himself and he never looked back. He and Cynthia were the parents of a five-year-old son, Kenneth, Jr. and an eleven-month-old daughter Taylor-Lynn. Secretly, Timothy admired the life his friend and his wife had and their blissful happiness sometimes had him longing for that kind of love. He'd had relationships over the years and a few had gotten pretty serious, but none to the point where he wanted to propose marriage.

A few times Cynthia tried to set him up with a friend or two of hers and it never went anywhere. Timothy always reached a certain part of being involved with a woman and then he would lose interest even though he knew the women were great. They had good jobs, nice personalities and were physically beautiful. He knew the problem wasn't them, but him. He loved women, especially sexy, gorgeous women, but he could never see himself in a committed relationship with plans of marriage and children. To him, those kinds of things only happened to other people; people who lived happy lives surrounded by family and friends.

"I'm good and I'm sorry about that. I didn't do much besides watch some football and get some projects done around my house. I appreciate the Thanksgiving dinner invitation and I was going to come by, but at the last minute, I really wanted to just enjoy some peace and quiet," he explained.

"We really hoped you'd change your mind and show up. You know Cynthia worries about you spending holidays alone," Kenneth said.

"I know and tell her I appreciate her thinking about me, but I'm fine. Since the staff had the weekend off, I stayed in and looked over some reports and completed the work on my kitchen backsplash, so it was a productive weekend. Today, it's back to business as usual."

"Okay, my friend. I won't pry too much. You know that Cynthia and I are here anytime you need us. Kenny made some Thanksgiving cutouts in school and he has one he wants to give you so get by here soon so he can give it to you. I offered to take it to you and he was adamant that he wanted to see the smile on your face when he gave it to you himself."

"I promise I'll get over to see them both soon. Make sure

you tell everyone I said hello and you and I need to get together for a poker game soon. I know you have new money that I need to separate you from," he quipped, lightening the mood of the conversation.

"Not on your life, pal. I'm hearing about all the business that's been coming your way lately and I think I need to unhand some of those funds from you. I agree, poker soon. I'm heading to the dealership. We'll get together before Christmas for the game."

"Sounds like a plan", Timothy said right before ending the call.

He appreciated how much his friends worried about him, but the things that always had him down, not even his friends could fix.

Timothy got up from his desk to close his office door to shut out the world. He turned and walked over to his window that looked out over the Chicago sky. He did something he'd never done before in his life. To no one in particular he said, "I'm not sure what I believe in, but I do believe that I wasn't supposed to live my whole life alone. If there is something or someone out there who can hear me, I hope you know that's from my heart. When will things turn around for me in my personal life as they have in my professional life? If I knew how to be more inviting, I would do it. A little help here would be good."

More lately than ever, whenever he talked to Kenneth and heard the stories about what was happening with his wife and kids lately, he yearned for that life, he yearned for that love. Would his past forever keep him from having a future that included a wife and children? He was his own worst enemy, not knowing how to get out of his own way and find happiness. The time was coming for him to stop blaming his past for his lack of thriving personally in his present and possibly his future. Perhaps, if the cards were dealt in his favor and somewhere, someone was looking out for him, he'd find a little more happiness in his life, especially around the holidays.

He shook off his melancholy mood and went back to his desk to look over the information on the new client that he would be speaking to soon. It was time to put off personal for a while and get down to business.

"Mr. Cornish, Jeffrey is here to see you per your request," Ariana said over the intercom.

"Send him in."

2

"Good morning, this is Holly Day. How can I help you?"

"Ms. Day, it's Mr. Watson, the attorney representing Ms. Wallace's estate. I'm glad I was able to catch you. I wanted to let you know that all of the paperwork went through without any problems. You should be hearing soon from the representative at TRC Realty who will be working with you to find a new house for the children's group home. Just remember, the stipulations of the will were very clear. The property must remain in the Chicago area and as long as you are still willing, the request was that you continue to stay on as the executive director. The only time that can change is if you hire your own replacement, if you one day need to leave the position," he said.

Holly was excited. It has been her life's work to help children that others would forget about and this new children's home will enable her to help even more.

"That's good news, Mr. Watson. I want to be sure that you know that I don't currently live at the house, but that I do hire the staff that live there around the clock attending to every need of every child who comes through our doors. Were you able to get that stipulation removed that I live there?" Holly asked, hopeful.

"Yes, I was. That was changed right before Ms. Wallace passed away. She understood that you may one day want to have a family of your own and didn't want the children to miss out on your leadership because of that part of the will. There is enough money left for the care of the children and to maintain the new home for many, many years to come. We thank you for your tireless efforts," Mr. Watson said.

Holly was overjoyed. Helping children was her mission in life and she took it seriously.

"Thank you. This money will be a huge relief because we weren't sure where the funding would come from to continue to operate the house. The state funding just wasn't enough anymore. I'm grateful to Ms. Wallace and appreciate that she thought of us enough to include us in her will."

"I agree. She's always been a supporter of several homes for children around Chicago and she was particularly interested in making sure that yours was funded especially for an expansion to assist even more children. Please call me if you have any questions or concerns."

Holly could barely contain her excitement after disconnecting the call. It's moments like this that gave her a reason to get up and come to work every day.

She enjoyed her job as a social worker for the city of Chicago and as the current executive director of the Open Care House, a home for children. She wished there was no need for places like the children's home, but she was glad that she was able to help them have a roof over their heads and food on the table. She made sure they each continued with their education, no matter their circumstances, knowing how important it would be to their success as adults.

She herself had been in foster care throughout her childhood and though her situation could have been a sad one, she made the best of it by keeping her head in her books and dreaming of the day that she would have her own home and family.

Now, she would happily wait on the call from TRC Realty who would help in her search for a larger home. She had a few she'd checked out on the internet that could be prospects for relocation of the current home. If the children had to be in a home, she wanted it to be the best possible one out there in the Chicago area and if she could bring more on board from other less appealing facilities, she wanted to do that sooner rather than later.

"Ms. Day?"

Holly's assistant appeared in the doorway of her office.

"Yes, Charlotte."

"Ms. Doris from Open Care House is here to see you with little Angel in tow. She said Angel didn't have a good night last night and that you told her to let you know the next time Angel had a sleepless night. Do you have time to see them now?"

Holly knew without a doubt, she had the time. She always made time for the children, especially Angel.

Angel came to the home from the courts after her mother and father gave her up because they decided drugs were more important to them than the welfare of their baby daughter. The parents claimed they had no family and because the system would rather see parents turn children into them than to leave them abandoned someplace, they happily took the baby to take care of her. They hoped the parents would get treatment and return, but they didn't. If she remembered correctly, Angel was less than a year old when she was brought in and was now five years old. She was the most precious little girl Holly had ever encountered. Angel was full of life and could sometimes be on the shy side until she really warmed up to you. She loved dolls and loved to have tea parties as she believed all little girls should do. She tried to spend time with each child, one on one throughout the month and when it was Angel's time, she always wanted to play tea party.

Just recently, Holly was notified that the parents had signed over all parental rights to the state and then again disappeared, so soon Angel would most likely be placed in foster care with a family while they held out hope that she would one day soon be adopted. Until that time, she would stay at the group home.

Angel's story wasn't much different than hers. She too had been given away by her parents at a very young age and was thankful that eventually things had turned out positive for her. It was her plan that Angel be united with a family as soon as possible. She'd spent enough time in an unsure situation.

Being around Angel had her wishing for children of her own. She knew that one day when she married, she hoped it was to a man who wanted lots of children with some being those they could adopt and give a good home to. There were many who needed that and she wanted to open her home to them, not as foster children, but as her own, adopted children. One day, Holly thought.

"Yes, show them in," she said.

Before she could get up to greet them at the door, Angel

came bounding through it and headed straight for her to give her a big hug, something Holly had gotten used to getting every time she saw her.

"Angel," she said with cheer, returning the little girl's hug.

"Hi, Holly."

Holly took her and and walked over to the sofa in her office.

"I hear you didn't sleep good last night. Were you sick?" she asked.

"I kept having bad dreams."

"Bad dreams?"

She looked up at Ms. Doris, one of the women who helped care for the children and who lived in residence at the home.

"Doris, why don't you take a break while I talk with Angel," she said.

"Of course, and I'll go grab a soda. Just let me know when you're done."

After Doris left, Holly turned her attention back to Angel.

"Now, what's this about a bad dream?" she asked.

"I had a bad dream that I went to live with a bad family who didn't really want me and they put me in a box," Angel explained.

"A box? Why would anyone put an Angel in a box?" Holly asked, smiling in hopes it would add a lighter tone to the conversation.

"That's what mean old Bobby said. I told him I was going to get a new mommy and daddy soon and he said that they would be mean and make me live in a box. You won't let them put me in a box will you Holly?" Angel asked with soft, pleading eyes as she turned her head to the side and looked up at her.

Holly's heart melted. How could anyone not want and love a child as precious as Angel, she thought.

"I wouldn't let anyone put you in a box and don't you listen to Bobby. I will talk to him when I come to the house later. That wasn't a nice thing for him to say and he was just trying to scare you. He didn't mean it, I'm sure and don't you believe him for one minute. I promise you that when we find you a new mommy and daddy, they will be the best mommy and daddy ever. No one will have a better mommy and daddy in the whole wide world than you," Holly said, convincing the little girl.

As soon as Angel perked up, she smiled. Nothing gave her more satisfaction than to see a smile on the face of every little child.

"Okay?" she asked.

"Okay, Holly."

Holly watched as the frown that Angel had while telling her the story was turned into the biggest smile, the kind that she always wanted to see.

"Good. Now, I'm going to go get Ms. Doris, so that you can go home and get some sleep to make up for the sleep you didn't get last night."

"I like coming to visit you, Holly. You always make me happy," Angel said.

"You make me happy, too," she admitted and meant it.

"Are you ready to go now?"

Angel nodded her head yes and pulled out her favorite doll to play with until Ms. Doris returned.

~~

"Jeffrey, have a seat," Timothy said when he appeared in

his office. Timothy opened the file for the client he wanted to discuss.

"I hear you want to take this account for yourself," Jeffrey said getting a glimpse of the file.

"Yes. I looked over the information this weekend and I think I know why they requested me. I have a history with children's homes and I think they feel I would have more interest than anyone in helping these children. I actually know the woman who left the money to the children's home. I once lived in a home that was once run by one of her sons. That was many years ago, and she's kept up with me because according to these notes, she specifically requested that the job of finding a replacement home was given to my company and that I be the one to handle it directly. I didn't realize that was the case when I assigned this one to you. I didn't want you to think there was any other reason why I was taking this one off of your plate and taking it over. Ariana has a list of new clients for you to choose from and though I tend to assign these, I want you to have first crack at them. You're one of my best on the staff and these new clients are some pretty heavy hitters. Again, I wanted to be sure you were okay with that and understood why we need to make a change," Timothy said.

"Of course, I understand and it's not a problem. Just let me know if you need my help on this one at all. You'll see in the file, I'd already looked into a few properties to go over with Ms. Day. I believe she's the person you'll be working with and she also has a list of places she wanted us to check into for her. I haven't done much on this, so it will be an easy transition back over to you," Jeffrey said.

"Sounds great. I'm actually going to have Ariana have her come in tomorrow to get the preliminary work done and I'll also share with her the few suggestions you've already noted. Great job on this," Timothy said.

"Happy to help in any way I can."

"You're an incredible asset to the TRC team."

"I also wanted to tell you thanks for the Thanksgiving bonuses you gave out. I was able to use mine to do some early Christmas shopping for the family on Black Friday," Jeffrey said.

"I'm glad it came in handy. All of you do great work and I want you to know how much I appreciate you. I may not always get the chance to say it, but I do," Timothy said.

"The entire team knows it."

"Now I don't want to hold you long. I just wanted to bring you up to date on what's going on and to see if you had any questions."

"No, I'm good. I'll stop by to see Ariana about the new client list and thanks for giving me first pick," Jeffrey said standing to leave.

"Let me know if there are any questions about that also," Timothy said just before Jeffrey was out of range to hear him.

Timothy went back to his desk and captured the name and number of the woman he would have Ariana reach out to. Apparently, Ms. Day would be the person making the final decision on the property. He looked forward to getting all of the information on the needs for the home and he would be sure each and every one of them was met. It was not only important for the welfare of the children who would be living there, but for him as well. He knew what it was like and though life at those homes had improved significantly over the years, he would rather see each and every child in a home, adopted by parents who loved them.

He had that dream, which never came true for him, but that didn't mean he wouldn't do all he could to help them. He didn't want any other child to experience the loneliness that he went through.

3

"Mr. Cornish, Ms. Day is here to see you," Ariana said appearing in his office doorway.

"I'm ready for her. Go ahead and show her in please," Timothy replied.

Ms. Day walked into his office as if she were walking on a cloud. His first sight of her took his breath away because she was beautiful. He was expecting an older woman, much like the type he'd seen on old movies who ran children's homes. Ms. Day was far from that. She smiled and brought the sunshine in the room with her. There was something ever-present about her and he was immediately drawn in like a moth to a flame. He couldn't remember a time when he'd been so intensely aware of a woman before.

His visitor enthralled him and she hadn't even said a word yet. Her beauty was magnetic and she was so impeccably dressed and her confidence showed, he was mesmerized.

She walked into his office in a red and black business suit that was as professional as they came, but at the same time, she was sexier than any woman he'd ever encountered. What caught his attention the most was the length of her neck which was more defined because she wore her hair pulled up. One feature he always loved on a woman was her neck and he could imagine nuzzling hers and feeling like he belonged there. Remembering why she was here, he stopped ogling her, cleared his throat so that he could concentrate and stood to greet her.

"Ms. Day," he said shaking her extended hand.

"Mr. Cornish, it's nice to meet you. Thank you for taking the time to meet with me today."

Timothy got lost in the soft, soothing sound of her voice. Never had any woman had such an immediate impact on him and he liked it.

"Let's have a seat at my conference table. Can I have Ariana get you some coffee or tea?" he asked.

"No, thank you," she replied.

"Ariana, hold all of my calls until after this meeting please," he said before grabbing the folder off of his desk.

"Mr. Cornish, before we get started, I want to let you know that the help you are giving to us with this project is life-saving. We've been in the current house for over ten years and before that, another organization had used it for the same purpose. The money donated to the new house will allow us to finally get a larger place to accommodate more children and provide more things like a computer room and a large activities room. I'm excited to work with your company."

"We are more than grateful that we were chosen to help you. Since we'll be working together on this, why don't you call me Timothy," he said.

He watched as her features softened and to him she glowed. He knew his mind should be on business, but his visitor was stunning and he was finding it hard to concentrate on business.

"I can do that Timothy, if you'll call me Holly," she said in response.

Timothy wasn't quite sure he heard what she said her name was. Couldn't be, he thought.

"Wait, what? Your first name is Holly?" he asked seeing the significance in her name.

"Yes. Is something wrong?" she asked.

"No, not at all. That would mean that your full name is Holly Day. It almost sounds like holiday."

When Holly smiled, Timothy couldn't help but smile back. He was sure she was thinking it wasn't the first time someone had made a reference to that.

"I get that a lot when people say my whole name. I guess when my mother gave birth to me, she thought it was cute, though I didn't grow up thinking it was cute. I was made fun of a lot as a child, but as an adult, I see how it is funny."

It seemed that neither knew what to say next. There was an intense and magnetic power in the air and both sensed it as their eyes connected and the air electrified.

Holly couldn't believe her reaction to the man sitting across from her. She tried her best to plaster a simple, business smile on her face, but inside she was struggling to catch her breath. Timothy Cornish was fine, tall and she didn't want to forget to say to herself that he was sexy beyond any man in the latest copy of every magazine with a male model on the cover. She discreetly watched him as he walked to his desk to grab a folder before joining her at the table and his presence overpowered her along with the sexy swagger of his walk. She loved a man who walked like he held the power, very strong and manly. Now as they sat staring at each other, a few spicy images crossed her mind, something that never happened to her. It was as if they were purposely being drawn to each other, almost as if they were meant to meet. She was feeling some type of way and it felt good. Did she believe in fate?

Timothy knew he was supposed to be doing something besides staring at Holly, but for the life of him, he couldn't figure out what it was. He was captivated by Holly and though he'd dated some beautiful women over the years, there was something sparkly about her. The air seemed to crackle around them with enough electricity to power a house.

House! That's what he was supposed to be doing. He should be talking about a house and not imagining what all that red in her suit would look like thrown about on the floor after he removed it from her body. Shaking off the thought, at least for now, he cleared his throat to bring his mind back to the business at hand.

"Why don't we talk a little about what some of your other wants are for the house besides space for a computer and activities room and I will be able to make additional recommendations."

"Sure," Holly said, still not taking her eyes off of his. He didn't appear to want to look away either, she realized. "I have a few properties I looked at on the internet. I brought information on those with me today if that will also help. Most of them had the necessary space that I'm looking for and all are within the dollar range for what's allowed."

Holly reached into her briefcase to retrieve the printouts for him.

"Thanks. That will help me a lot in determining just what to look for."

As he reached for the papers she was handing him, their hands touched and he felt a shock. Timothy knew she felt it as well because she quickly let go of the papers and he saw the look of shock on her face that he knew mirrored his own. He tried to keep his thoughts on business and failed at that attempt. He looked her in the eyes.

"You felt that too?" he asked, brazenly.

Holly hesitated before replying. She had felt it, but didn't think they'd be discussing it. What she felt wasn't just a shock like you get from being on carpet and touching someone, but it was as if for a brief moment, she saw them together, happy without a care in the world. It was a feeling you get when you realize that something or someone had a hand in two people meeting. It was the kind of feeling you get when you get a sure sign that you were meant to be in this moment together and recognizing each other for something other than just work purposes.

Holly cleared her throat while also hoping to focus.

"Yes, I felt it. What was that? It wasn't just an electric shock, Timothy."

Holly said his name in a way that made his heart rate speed up and his manhood jump. It felt like it was about to leap out of his pants and jump across the table right into her. He had to be crazy, he thought. He had known Holly for only a few minutes and he wanted her. With as lovely as she was, any man would be lying if he said he didn't want to make slow passionate love to her and he would not be an exception to that. He wanted her to be his and it was as if something as at work to make sure he knew it.

"I don't know what that was, but I'm glad I wasn't the only one who felt it," he said.

"No, you weren't," she whispered softly.

Throwing her for a loop, an image popped in her head of them standing before a room full of their family and friends about to commit their lives to each other. She was dressed in a long, flowing white gown and he was dressed handsomely in a black tuxedo, looking amazing. What kind of angel is having a hand in what was happening between them?

Holly had dated men over the years and one in particular for a few years, but none had ever had the impact on her like Timothy was having. Some kind of force was at work here and it wasn't playing games. Something wanted them both to experience the instant attraction and not forget it. From the looks Timothy was giving her, she wasn't the only one with that thought.

~~

Holly and Timothy talked for over an hour and once their meeting was done, they were happy that they had some great prospects for properties. Now, it was time for her to leave and Holly wasn't sure she wanted to.

"Well, let me thank you for all that you're doing. I feel good about the properties you were able to pull up and let me look at. Adding in the ones I gave you earlier, I think one of these will be the one. Many of them had everything we would need for the children, plus more. I can't wait to visit them," Holly said.

"I'm glad to hear that. I'll make some calls today and let you know what I come up with. I think I should have some showing times set up by the end of the week. Why don't we get together in a few days and narrow down which ones are true prospects?" Timothy asked.

"That's sounds like a great idea. Whatever day works for you, I will be sure and clear my schedule."

"What about Thursday around the same time as today?" he asked.

"Thursday works for me," she agreed.

Holly had to smile at both of their attempts to prolong their time together. Eventually she would have to leave and she didn't want to overstay her welcome knowing he probably had more clients to see.

Timothy watched as Holly got up to leave and he knew that he wanted to see her outside of work and it was now or never. Now that the work talk was over, he wanted to move on to something else and hoped the vibes he was getting from her matched his own.

"Holly, if I'm crossing any kind of line here, tell me so and I'll apologize, but I was hoping now that the work discussion is over, I could interest you in having dinner with me?" he stumbled out.

Holly's heart leaped. She wanted to know that he was talking personal and not business.

"Is this to talk more about the house hunt?" she asked.

"Only if that's what you want to talk about, but that wouldn't be my preference if you say yes. I'm not normally this aggressive when I first meet a woman, but from the moment you walked in my office, I have barely been able to concentrate on work. I think you're a beautiful woman and sitting here for this past hour or so, I find myself wanting to know more about you that doesn't involve house hunting. Would you be interested in putting our work hats to rest and get to know each other a little better?"

Timothy wasn't sure he was breathing as he waited for her response. She didn't appear to be insulted and he watched for any dissention in her facial expression. He saw none and hoped that would lead to a positive end to their meeting.

"I'd like that and I have to admit, you're not the only one who had thoughts that had nothing to do with house hunting the moment I walked in. This is certainly out of character for me to have such an instantaneous attraction to someone, especially when I'm talking business," she admitted.

"Well, I say that's a sign that we should pursue this further. Do you agree?" he asked, hopeful.

"Yes, I do," Holly said softly and decided to wait until she got to her car to shout her excitement. What was it about this man that had her acting like a school girl who had just been asked to the prom, she thought.

"What about Friday night for dinner?"

"I'd love that. Friday for dinner would be nice," she said without hesitation. There was no stopping her now. From the moment she walked into Timothy's office, she knew that the feeling of interest was mutual and there was no way she would deny it by thinking too hard about going out to dinner with him.

"Great. It's a date and I'm looking forward to it. I know you have all of my business information, but I want to give you my personal number in case something comes up," he said reaching into his pocket to withdraw a business card. He wrote his home and cell number on the back and handed it to her.

"I'll put these in my cell phone when I get to my car and I'll dial you so that you have my number in your phone. Does that work for you?" she asked.

It more than worked for him.

"It works better than you think."

Timothy was more ready for their date than he'd ever

been for any of date in his life. This incredible woman agreed to have dinner with him and he already felt like the luckiest man in the world.

Holly turned to leave and then stopped and turned back around.

"Thank you again for helping and for asking me out for Friday."

"There is something that made me feel like I would be missing out on the chance of a lifetime if I let you leave here today without asking you out on a date. I seriously felt compelled to do it as if my life depended upon it. Does that sound crazy?" he asked.

"Not at all. I was actually thinking while we talked that if you hadn't asked me out by the time I got up to leave, I was going to ask you to dinner. I've never done that before, but like you, something came over me, compelling me to also make sure I didn't leave here without testing the water to see if the attraction was mutual."

Her boldness surprised her. It was as if the spark felt when they touched breathed new life into her and it felt good.

"Oh, it's mutual and I intend to continue to discover just how much," he said.

Holly shivered slightly at the huskiness in his voice. She needed to leave now before she burst into flames in the middle of his office. Suddenly, she felt warm.

Now that their business was over for the day, Timothy escorted her to the door of his office.

"I'll give you a call about those properties before the end of the day," he said out loud making sure to use his business voice. There was no need in alerting his assistant about the side conversation he and Holly had been having.

"I look forward to hearing from you," Holly said as she exited the building, walking past Timothy as he held the door open for her.

Once Holly was gone, Timothy stood in his doorway, not sure of what just happened. In just one short hour of being in her presence and for most of it, talking about business, he'd met the most incredible woman he'd ever come across in his life and if he didn't know any better, he could say he'd just fallen in love.

He thought back to the moment earlier in the day when he stood at the window in his office and spoke to no one in particular, almost begging for some help in finding focus in his personal life. A few short hours later, a woman walks in and from that moment on, everything in his life seemed crystal clear. Not only that, but for the first time in his life, he felt as hopeful about his personal life as he did about his work life. That was major for him.

He silently thanked whatever powers were listening to his earlier plea. He was embracing the surprising change in his circumstance and since he asked for it, he would see where it led. He didn't realize he was still standing and staring at the last place he'd seen Holly standing before she left his office until Ariana asked him if he needed something.

"What? Did you say something?" he asked, trying to focus.

"Yes. You were still standing in the doorway a good five minutes after Ms. Day left and I thought maybe you wanted something."

"No, I'm good. Actually, I'm great and tell everyone I'm buying lunch today. I know we have a few people out showing properties today, so let's make sure we order enough so that when they return, they can enjoy it too," he said in a light-hearted voice that even shocked him.

He shocked himself at how good he was feeling. He caught a glimpse of the surprise look on Ariana's face and smiled. It wasn't as if he had never bought lunch for the staff before, but in the past, it was always planned ahead of time and it was usually for some type of celebration.

"Are we celebrating something I forgot to tell everyone about?" she asked.

"No, I'm just in the lunch buying mood today."

"Is that a smile I see on your face for no reason at all or is something going on I shouldn't know about or ask about?" Ariana asked.

Timothy looked at her and smiled brighter.

"Are you fishing for information?" he quipped.

"Only if you're going to tell me what threw you in such a good mood all of a sudden. Could it perhaps have been that beautiful woman that just walked out of here?"

Timothy laughed out loud.

"Yeah, you're fishing, but I'm not biting," he said turning to go back in his office.

"Okay, Mr. Cornish. You had me worried there for a minute. I was about to call the police and tell them that I think you may have been replaced by the body snatchers or something," she said, laughing.

Timothy laughed along with her knowing she was on to something. He hadn't been replaced by a body snatcher, but he wasn't the same person he was when he arrived. He had a date with a beautiful woman in a few days and he had a feeling, it was going to be the best date he'd ever had. He'd had a sudden transformation and Ms. Holly Day was the reason.

There was something in that touch, he thought to himself.

"Let's do Jay's Deli and just order a wide variety and see how soon they can deliver," he said before sitting down. He already knew he wasn't going to get much work done because all he could think about was Holly.

~~

Holly sat in her car without putting the key in the ignition and wondered what had just happen. She exhaled as if she had been holding her breath for a long time. From what she could remember before the love train hit her, she had come to the offices of TRC Realty today to talk about work and came out with a date for Friday night. She wasn't complaining and she was in fact, happier about seeing him outside of work that she could have imagined she would be. Everything happened so fast, it was almost scary. Scary or not it felt right. Whatever it was, she was ready for it. Timothy was some man and in the back of her mind, she was also saying, he was her man!

Finally pulling out into traffic, she thought back to when the last time she'd been out on a date. Work had completely consumed her time and having a personal life had somehow taken a back seat to everything else. When she was younger, she would day dream about the right man finding her, getting married and having a house full of kids. Back then her plan was to already be halfway there, but her life had taken a different turn and it was one she knew she needed to take because of the kids she encountered everyday. As much as she would like to have someone, the kids needed someone too and it was her life's mission to find a happy home for every child that she came in contact with that had a need.

Holly smiled as she drove along wondering if fate had played a hand in her meeting and immediately being enchanted by Timothy. She knew absolutely nothing about him other than he was handsome and she was enthralled by him. The excitement she felt when they briefly touched and felt a jolt, she knew meeting him was no coincidence. The date on Friday, she already knew, would not be a regular date. The stars were aligning and they were cascading all around her.

Excitement over Friday had her thinking of what she wanted to do to prepare. She wanted to get her hair and nails done and perhaps buy herself a new sexy dress for the evening. She was already feeling like Friday was going to be a night like none she'd ever experienced before. She had a feeling Timothy was a man like none she'd ever met before. She was thinking of what would be a good day to get all of that done when her phone played the ringtone 'Who Run the World', by Beyoncé, a ringtone reserved for her best friend, Teresa.

"Hey girl. What are you doing and where have you been? I've been calling you for the past half hour," Teresa said.

"I had a business meeting this morning about the new property and I turned my ringer off. I told you about it a few weeks ago. Remember I told you about the money we were getting to find a bigger, better place? What's up?" Holly asked.

"Nothing really. I wanted to see if you wanted to have lunch today if you were free."

"Yes, I'm free. If anyone has the same food obsession as you, it's definitely me. I can't wait to tell you about the properties we talked about his morning and to tell you about a man I just met. I think I'm already in love."

Holly braced herself for Teresa's reaction. If anyone else knew about her lack of a dating life, it was her best friend.

"What? You just met a man? Where? What man? Who? When? You know the rundown and I want to hear it all!" Teresa exclaimed.

"Okay, that's a lot of words with a lot of question marks behind them. I'll answer them all over lunch, I promise."

"Wow, he must be some guy. I've never heard you talk like that about a guy right after you met him. Yeah, we definitely need to do lunch because I want to hear all about this man and don't you dare think about leaving anything out. I'll see you at the spot at noon."

"I'll be there," Holly said hanging up and smiling like she'd just won the lottery. To her, she had.

4

Timothy paced back and forth in his office waiting for Holly to arrive. It was the day before their date and they were scheduled to go out and look at a few houses he selected that he thought would be what she was looking for along with the few she'd provided to him.

He couldn't wait to see her again. They'd spoken by phone several times about work and then they shifted into conversations that were more about who they each were and what they thought about the connection mutually felt when they first met. He didn't mention the conversation he had out loud to himself before she had arrived earlier in the week. He didn't want to chalk it up to his wish for personal success like he'd reached in his business life. So far today, he'd yawned three times after being up until the middle of the night talking to her. Even though they both had work in the morning, neither were ready to get off the phone. That was a first for him and talking to her was as comfortable as if he'd been talking to a friend he'd had for years. He was most excited about the fact that Holly had been in the foster care system just like he had and so they had a lot in common. She understood him like no other woman he'd ever dated before had.

Timothy checked his clock again. He still had about an hour before Holly was due to arrive. Why was he pacing so nervously already, he thought to himself.

"Mr. Cornish," Ariana said interrupting his thoughts of Holly.

"Yes, Ariana," he looked up and replied, realizing she'd caught him pacing.

"Well, first is something wrong? You're pacing around."

"No everything is fine," he said, trying to play off what he was really thinking about.

"Okay, well, Mr. Kenneth is here to see you. He said he knows he didn't have an appointment, but he wanted to talk to you if you were free."

"Of course. Tell him to come right in."

At least with Kenneth here, he could temporarily get his mind off of his excitement over seeing Holly again.

"Timothy, my man," Kenneth said when he entered.

"Hey, what's up?" Timothy asked.

"Nothing. Cynthia pushed me to deliver this cheesecake she baked for you since you didn't show up for Thanksgiving dinner last week. Of course, I ate the original one she baked for you and she made this one fresh last night. I figured I better get it to you before I'm tempted to eat this one too."

Timothy laughed out loud.

"Don't even think about it. Your wife makes the best cheesecake."

Cynthia knew how much he loved butter brittle cheesecake. It was a flavor she made from scratch only for him.

"You know I was tempted all the way here in the car!" Kenneth jested.

"Thanks. I'll call and thank her later," Timothy said.

"So, what's going on with you? I have a few minutes."

"Nothing really. Just work, work and then more work. I have a client coming in a few that I'm taking out to show some properties to."

"You're still taking people out on visits? I thought you left showings to members of your staff."

"It was a stipulation in a will that I be the one to handle this personally. It's for a children's group home. They're looking to relocate and I'm showing the representative a few selections today," he replied.

"Cool. I see business is still growing by leaps and bounds. You've hired a few more people. I noticed the extra staff when I came in."

"We can hardly keep up with the demand. I'm planning to hire a few more after the holiday season."

"What are your plans for Christmas? Cynthia is planning something, but I don't know what yet. I'm sure it will involve a friend or two of hers who just happens to be single. You know she will never stop trying to get you married."

Timothy shook his head from side to side. Cynthia has been trying to hook him up with the perfect woman for a long time. He's glad it hasn't worked because he believed he'd just met the woman of his dreams earlier in the week.

"Your wife is amazing and all, but she really needs to stop doing that. Those poor girls come under the pretense that I was aware and in actuality, I was being setup just like they were."

"I know, but you know she wants everyone to be as blissfully happy as she and I are. She thinks you avoid some of her gatherings because you typically come without a date. I keep telling her you can get your own dates, but she doesn't listen to met at all."

"Well, tell her if she has something for Christmas this year, I may come and if I do I'll be showing up with a date."

Kenneth looked at him sideways as if he was waiting to hear more.

"Are you dating someone you haven't told me about?" Kenneth asked.

Cat was out of the bag, Timothy thought.

"Not exactly."

He knew Kenneth could read him like a book and no way was he going to get away without explaining himself.

"Are we going to play twenty questions or are you going to spill it?"

Timothy walked around and sat down behind his desk. The last thing he wanted to do was to start pacing again as soon as he started thinking about Holly.

"I met someone," he said nonchalantly.

He laughed when Kenneth waved him off.

"You met someone? Okay, you met someone. I know you man and you're always meeting someone. Who is this one a model, an actress, some woman who did flips and acrobatics in bed? One thing I know about you that maybe a lot of other people don't know because you try to be private, but I know about your noncommittal dating lifestyle, to put it in mild terms. There's nothing wrong with that and every man single and married is jealous over the number of women you meet without even trying. They flock to you like a snake to a snake charmer."

Timothy waited while Kenneth had a good laugh before putting his serious face on.

"You didn't hear me, Ken. I said I *met* someone."

This time he saw the moment Kenneth knew how serious he was.

No one said anything for a few seconds before Kenneth finally understood what he said and leaned back in the chair, crossed his legs so that he could focus. Timothy knew the moment Kenneth realized he wasn't speaking of some average woman he met and bedded.

"Oh, you mean you *met* someone," he said, putting special emphasis on the word met.

Timothy wanted complete privacy, so he got up quickly and closed his office door after telling Ariana to let him know if Holly arrived early before he'd finished with Kenneth.

He came back around and sat at his desk again and this time, the serious look on his face forced Kenneth to take stock in the no-laughing matter conversation they were about to have.

"Who is she and where did you meet her?"

"Well, her name is Holly and I met her right here in my office. She's the client I'll be showing properties to today. I met her right here and the moment she walked through that door, I've been in love with her ever since."

"Wow, this is deep my friend, you just said the love word. Start from the beginning because I've never, ever heard you say the word love before and never when making reference to a woman. Besides that, this is someone you've just met and from the moment you saw her you were in love? This must be some woman," Kenneth said.

"Oh yeah, she is."

Timothy gave Kenneth a run down on what occurred the day he met Holly including the energy he felt when he touched her that seemed to breathe new life into him.

"Tim, this is great man and I have got to meet this woman."

"So, you don't think I'm crazy or losing my mind talking about being in love with a woman I barely know anything about and I've only met once?" Timothy asked.

"Not at all. I've known you for a few years and I know how to read you. Right now, I'm reading that this is coming from the heart. You've met this woman and you're in love with her, which is called love at first sight and I don't doubt it one bit."

Timothy exhaled. This was the first time he'd said his honest feelings for Holly out loud and when he said it to himself, he thought he sounded crazy considering he literally just met the woman and they hadn't even been out on their first date yet. He knew hardly anything about her beyond the things they'd shared during their late-night conversations, but he knew from the first moment, he was in love. He knew Kenneth was shocked, but so was he.

"I haven't told you the best part. You know how I'm always walking around like the Grinch, especially around holidays? You will never guess what her name is," he said, still not believing it himself.

He didn't wait for Kenneth to guess, he blurted it out.

"Her name is Holly Day."

He waited for a response beyond the look of sheer humor on Kenneth's face.

"Are you serious?" Kenneth said, surprised.

"Man, I couldn't write something this good for a movie if I tried. I don't think anyone could. I am dead serious.

That is her actual name. Can you imagine that? I'm the biggest humbug there is and the woman I already proclaim to love is named Holly Day. I know it sounds crazy, like some Christmas movie or something, but it's not. This actually happened to me."

Timothy was shocked to hear himself say it. A woman he couldn't stop thinking about was named Holly Day. For him, that was saying something.

"Tim, dude, this is some good stuff. Someone is looking out for you man, trying to make sure you are reading the signals loud and clear," Kenneth added.

"That's exactly what I'm thinking. I told you about my little chat at the window to myself. Right after that, things changed and I met Holly. It's not strange that the woman I would fall in love with at first sight would be named Holly Day. Can you believe I said I'm in love with this woman? I asked her out to dinner tomorrow night and she accepted right away. We both sense something is going on here and are anxious to see what it is."

"I'm serious when I say I can't wait to meet this woman. She must really be something special."

Kenneth exhaled loudly.

"You have no idea," he admitted.

"You're right, Mr. Grinch, I can already see a change in you. I've known you a lot of years, seen you go through a lot of women and have lived vicariously through your many adventures with them, but never have I seen this Timothy and I must say, I like it."

They both looked at the phone when Ariana chimed in via the phone intercom system.

"Mr. Cornish, Ms. Day has arrived for your meeting," Ariana could be heard through the intercom.

"Seems like you'll get your chance right now," Timothy said getting up to open his office door.

Timothy's smile could be seen from miles away as he couldn't control his immediate feeling of exuberance at seeing her. She was even more beautiful than she was the day he'd first met her.

When she entered, Kenneth could have sworn he saw a glow surrounding her very presence. He got a weird feeling that told him that this was some woman and exactly what his friend needed.

Kenneth and Timothy had been friends a lot of years and he always wanted the best for him. He knew Timothy's history and that he didn't have any family. Kenneth and his wife tried hard to always make him feel like family to them.

He watched as Holly entered Timothy's office and his friend lit up like a Christmas tree.

"Holly, I'd like you to meet Kenneth. He's the best friend any man could have," Timothy said introducing them.

"Hello," she said cheerfully.

"Kenneth, this is Holly Day. She is the executive director of the Open Care House children's home and I'm helping her find a new property for them to move into."

"Nice to meet you," Holly said, taking the hand Kenneth was extending to her.

"I feel like I already know you," he said looking to Timothy, signaling him that he was impressed already.

Holly looked at Timothy and smiled.

"Well, I hope it's all been good," she said.

"Oh, it's all been great. I'm going to leave so that you two can get your work done. It was a pleasure to meet you Holly and I hope to see you again," Kenneth said turning to leave.

"Likewise, Kenneth," Holly replied.

Timothy followed behind Kenneth and shut the door, leaving him and Holly in his office alone.

He turned back to her.

"Hello," was all he could think to say. He wasn't shocked when his reaction to her was just like it had been the first day they'd met. Her presence absorbed the entire room. She seemed to be everywhere, even all around him.

"Hi," she replied. "It's good to see you again."

Holly stood waiting for him to ask her to sit or to say something else. Instead, she was treated to a penetrating stare that told her that he'd been thinking about her as much as she'd been thinking about him. She could tell from his stare that he was as happy to see her as she was to see him. She thought about nothing, but him all day and the closer she got to his office, the more excited she became.

Timothy couldn't say another word. He was afraid something stupid would come out of his mouth if he did. Instead, he looked at his watch. She was twenty minutes early.

"I'm sorry. Am I too early? Did I disturb you?" she asked, concerned when he still hadn't said anything. She notice him checking his watch.

"No, not at all," he finally said.

"Are you sure? You look a little dazed," she added.

"You're not too early. In fact, I was wondering if we could actually begin our meeting at the exact time we planned."

Holly was confused. He said she wasn't too early, but he didn't want to start their meeting yet.

"Would you like for me to step back out into your

waiting area?" she asked, preparing to turn back around.

Timothy needed to say more because this was about to go wrong. He felt like a blundering idiot around her, he was so nervous. His words weren't matching his thoughts.

"No, that's not what I meant. I said that because I was hoping we could have a non-business moment before we jump into business mode if that's okay with you," he said, clearer this time.

Holly was relieved. She wasn't sure how to take his comment about starting the meeting at the actual agreed upon time.

She smiled, happy to know he was glad to see her and not just for business.

"What did you have in mind?" she asked comfortably.

Timothy didn't speak. He didn't want to ruin the moment or keep himself from doing exactly what he dreamed about all week. Before he changed his mind, he reached for her briefcase and sat it on his desk. When he turned back around, he pulled her into his arms and while holding his breath from being so overwhelmed by not just her beauty, but by her mere existence, he leaned closer and closer to her beautiful face. He moved slowly just in case he was moving too fast at wanting to kiss her and she was thinking otherwise. She apparently wasn't thinking otherwise because the moment she realized what he was about to do, Timothy felt her move tighter and closer into his embrace and up on her toes, just as eager for the kiss as he was. He didn't make either of them wait long.

The moment his lips touched hers lightly, that same electric charge he felt earlier in the week when they lightly touched each other happened again, but this time on a much larger scale. The feeling was just as welcomed now as it had been then. The spark didn't cause them to break away; it caused them both to lean even more into the kiss intoxicating kiss. Though the touch of their lips was soft as he caressed first her top lip and then her bottom, it caused an electric current to flow through his body. He felt like he was coming alive for the very first time. The feel of her body close to his and the delicious way she tasted, he took the kiss a little deeper when Holly parted her lips slightly and he went in search of her tongue.

The world around them disappeared as the kiss grew more intense on a level unmatched to anything he'd ever experienced. His body roared to life from how skillfully Holly was mating with his tongue. The moment the kiss went from soft and sexy to wild and brazen, Timothy didn't feel like he was in control. Holly was a master at getting what she wanted from a kiss and he willingly gave it to her while pulling everything from her she threw his way in the kiss.

Holly's tongue tasted sweet, which he knew was a combination of her and the sweet taste of her soft, silky lip gloss. Timothy tried to gather his breath in between plunges into her mouth, but he just wanted more and more and breathing became secondary. A power bigger than him had taken over and he was devouring her just as she was doing to him. Their mouths were mating like this would be the last kiss they would ever share. If he had anything to do with it, this was only the beginning.

Holly was out of breath. The moment Timothy's lips had touched hers, she held her breath in. She didn't want to focus on breathing; her only thoughts were on how good his lips felt making love to her mouth. When she was able to pull away for a mere second to take in another breath, she said his name on a whisper and the response she got from him was a grunt as he delved back in to mate with her mouth again. Over and over he plunged in and again and again she received him. She could stand here and do this all day, she thought. Her body already felt like it was about to shatter into a million little pieces. This kiss was more than anything she could have dreamed of or expected. When Timothy finally pulled back and looked at her, she knew that he was looking at her lips that she was sure had that look of just being thoroughly ravished. She didn't mind at all as she touched her lips with her finger where his had just been, already missing the feel of him.

"Wow!" she said when she could find her breath.

"Wow, is right!" Timothy added.

"I've never been kissed so thoroughly before," she admitted.

"I hope I wasn't too forward Holly," Timothy said, holding her attention with a lust-filled stare after being able to breathe again.

"No, not at all," she said, still rubbing her finger across her own lips. They still tingled as if they were still kissing.

"I've been thinking about doing that since the moment I met you. I wasn't sure I'd be able to focus on business today if I didn't first get that out of the way," he explained further, still trying to catch his breath.

"If you were forward, I was forward right along with you. I loved it and I wanted it just as much as you did. Now, maybe I'll be able to focus on work today, too and not think about how good it would feel to be in your arms, being kissed senseless like you just did," Holly said.

Timothy smiled knowing he couldn't wait to do it again. This was definitely the beginning of something marvelous.

"Senseless huh?" he asked and smiled brightly.

"Yes, senseless. I'm glad I still have a few minutes to get my thoughts in order before we move from personal to business. I hope we'll take time to visit personal again after business is done for the day," she boldly proclaimed.

Timothy was thinking the same thing.

"That can most definitely be arranged. I'm right there with you," he replied.

"I guess we need to move on to the work part of this," she said, not because she wanted to work, but because she wanted to get to the point where work would be in the rear-view mirror of their visit.

"Now, since I'm sure I've lost a few brain cells with that kiss, give me a minute to remember where I placed the file, so that we can talk about the properties we're going to look at today."

"I'll take a seat at the table. I think that kiss stole my ability to stand. A weak in the knees kiss is just what a woman needs right before a work meeting," Holly said seductively while going to take a seat on wobbly legs.

~~

"I loved each of the houses Timothy," Holly said as they were driving back to his office.

"Yeah, I have to admit that they were all really great properties and would serve your needs well," he said.

"I agree that any one of those would do. The locations are perfect and all had plenty of room and not just for the bedrooms for the children, but also for the common areas. I have a lot to think about," she said.

Timothy was happy that she was happy. It gave him great joy to see her smile so brightly.

"I'm glad you liked them. Now, of course, there are still

others that we can also look at if you want or you can make your decision from the three we saw today," Timothy said.

"I think I'll be able to decide from those three. Too many options would probably drag this out forever and those kids need a bigger house. I'm hoping to get everything completed and moved in after the first of the year. I want the kids to start the New Year off in a new home," she said before changing her mood from happy to sort of somber.

Timothy took note of the change in her as he looked over at her.

"What's wrong, Holly? Your mood went from a happy, smiling one to a frown," he inquired.

Holly knew he could see the change in her. She loved that she had just visited one of three homes for the kids and though it will help, it wasn't her ultimate goal. She had an even greater expectation.

"Oh, I'm sorry. You saw that?" she asked.

"Yes, I did. What were you thinking?" he said with concern.

Holly hesitated before saying anything that would make her seem ungrateful. She felt like she could trust Timothy with her inner most thoughts. They were becoming close and after several late-night phone conversations, she felt like she could tell him anything and he would support her.

"I appreciate the endowment that was left for the children to move them into a fantastic new home. My true wish is would be to find a great home for each and every child there and have that house remain empty because there would be no children in need of a group home. We have fourteen children right now, living in the current home and though we try our best to make sure each one knows they are loved, I know personally that there is nothing like having a family to be with each day, especially holidays like Christmas which is coming up in just a few weeks. I spend every Christmas at the house with the kids and thanks to a lot of business throughout Chicago, the kids get up Christmas morning to a room full of presents. To see their happy smiles always make my day. That day, none are thinking about being adopted or deal with issues of why they had parents who no longer wanted them or through circumstances beyond their control, could no longer care for them. All they know is that it's Christmas and they have toys. My wish every year is for them all to have families who want to adopt them and love them as if they were theirs from birth."

"That's a mighty big wish and I can see that you care a great deal for the kids. They are lucky to have someone like you and the others who work at the group home. It takes a special person to do what you are doing," he said.

Holly decided to go even further to explain.

"I grew up in foster homes, Timothy. I moved around so much that it was hard to get close to any one family. I never knew when I would be moved to a different one so yes, I know what it feels like as a child to want a family because I experienced the same thing. I also remember what it felt like the day I was adopted because it was the happiest day of my life. I want that feeling for each of them. It's heartbreaking when one of the kids asks us when we will find a family for them. It makes me want to cry every time. I wish that I could do more," she said.

Timothy understood and felt the depth of her feelings. He now knew why they had such a connection. They had even more in common than he thought.

"Holly I understand how you feel. I grew up in a home just like what you run for those kids. For years, I've tried to forget about those times in my life that were not happy or filled with cheer, especially around the holidays. I also knew what it felt like to not have a family of my own like a lot of those kids are feeling every day. Truth be told, I still know what that feels like even though I'm a grown man now. I know how much you want something different for those children and somehow, I get the feeling it will happen for each and every one of them. Until now, I didn't realize how much I'd like that for them as well. Maybe the same fate that brought you to me will see that this wish of ours also comes true," he said, looking over at her as they were stopped at a light, seeing the glow return once again to her face. That's what he needed to see. Seeing her smiling is what made his world bright.

"Thank you, Timothy. I needed to hear that and continue to believe that there is a family for each of them. We do share a special bond. We have both been where these children are now and perhaps we can come up with something if we put our heads together."

He nodded.

"Perhaps we can," he said.

5

Teresa was making a big fuss over Holly's makeup and jewelry and Holly was going crazy. It's not like she's never been out on a date before.

"Girl, you know I sell jewelry and I'm the jewelry queen. Trust me when I say this necklace and earring set will be spectacular with that sexy little black dress you're wearing tonight for your date with Mr. Wonderful!" Teresa exclaimed.

Holly put down the necklace she was thinking of and picked up the one Teresa suggested. When she held it up to see what it would look like around her neck, she decided Teresa was right. The necklace and earrings would be perfect. It was taking her too long to decide ad she knew it was due to the fact that her date night with Timothy was finally here and she was ready.

"You're right. I do love it and I'm going to wear this one. Now to pick out my shoes," she said, rummaging through her disorganized closet.

"Holly, you really need to let me come over and organize your life, especially your closet. You have the best shoe collection any girl could have, but you can't enjoy it when they're all over the bottom of your closet," Teresa pleaded.

"I know and you're right. Anytime other than tonight

would be good. I swear, I can keep all other parts of my life in order, but not my shoe collection. Even though it's crazy, I can still find everything I need, when I need it," she hooted.

"Okay, that's fair. I'll be over tomorrow, first thing. Well, that is if you come home tonight or if you don't have company in the morning," Teresa snickered, drawing Holly's attention away from shoe hunting.

"Shut your mouth, Teresa. I'm coming home tonight, alone," Holly said.

She knew what she'd said, but it certainly wasn't what she had planned. She'd already packed a small toiletry bag with some essentials just in case things happen to go to the next level tonight with Timothy. She didn't want to hold back anything and the way they were all over each other in his office the day before, if he was ready for the next level, she didn't want to hold back. She'd never felt the way she was feeling about Timothy. They had only known each other for less than a week, but whatever was happening between them was powerful and she was all-in. She knew without a doubt they were meant to be together and to her, there was no sense in wasting any time. She had a feeling Timothy was thinking the same thing. What she wouldn't do was tell Teresa anything about that. There were some secrets even the closest friends shouldn't know about.

"Okay, okay, I'm just saying. I won't come by early in the day. I'll wait until close to evening, you know, just in case," she said sporting a sly grin as if she could foresee the night with Timothy leading into something romantic.

Holly looked at her sideways.

"How about I call you when I'm free?" Holly suggested. She didn't want to say too much, but she also didn't want

Teresa showing up at a bad time.

"Let's do that and besides, I have plans of my own tonight. I may be the one preoccupied tomorrow," Teresa said in a sinister way.

"Oh, you and the mister are hanging tonight, huh?" Holly asked.

Teresa was in a loving relationship with a great man and Holly could appreciate the big smile on her face as she thought about him.

"Girl, you know that man can't resist me. I'm his morning noon and night and he certainly is mine. Why don't you send up the bat signal if the coast is clear? If I don't hear from you, I'll assume the date went extremely well and you have the necessary precautions in that little bag I saw when I came in."

Holly tried to looked surprised as if she didn't have a clue what she was talking about, but they had been friends long enough for her to not even try denying it.

Don't try to come back with that innocent look of yours," Teresa said when she was about to do just that.

Holly turned back to her closet and broke eye contact.

"Whatever girl," she said, playing it off.

"Remember I know you. Just have fun because you deserve this. If that man feels about you the way you feel about him in less than a week, I'd say do you girl!"

"That's just what I plan to do, so help me finish with getting ready. Timothy will be here any minute to pick me up," Holly said, now hurriedly moving about.

"You know I've never, ever seen you act this way about another guy before. Not even Russell who I was sure you were going to marry."

Holly thought about that and realized she had never felt

this way about any other man, not even Russell.

"Russell and I had fun, but I don't think we ever really had a deep connection. He was fun to be around and the sex was great, but there wasn't really a spark. With Timothy, the spark is off the meters. The minute I saw him, I felt like we were meant to meet and get to know each other."

"Sounds like it and I'm happy for you and besides, I didn't like Russell that much, but I have a feeling, I'm going to love Timothy like a brother."

"I could tell you and Russell didn't like each other. He was too possessive and didn't want me to have any friends. He thought single friends would lead to more fun with single men than he wanted. It was over before it started, but like I said, he was fun at the time, but Timothy, on the other hand, is much more than that."

"I can tell and I'm just as excited about the possibility as you are, so let's get you ready so that I can get out of here."

~~

Timothy had been on cloud nine all day. He couldn't count the number of times someone on his staff commented on the change in him, something they all apparently liked. He thought to himself that he must really have been a Grinch if he got this many compliments on the change in his personality for the past few days. He didn't want to tell them that the change was because of Holly. He knew it was all due to the woman in his life that he couldn't wait to be sitting across the table from having dinner with tonight. He wanted to also suggest that they perhaps take in a movie afterward because he already knew he didn't want the evening to end after dinner.

He was finally pulling up to her house after checking to

be sure he had the correct address. Her house was a beautiful brownstone with lots of outer charm and appeal. Being in the housing industry, a house spoke a lot about a person. He found a parking spot and walked up to the door. After pushing the door bell, he waited a few minutes and lost his ability to speak when Holly opened the door and stood before him looking even more beautiful than the other times he'd seen her. To him, each time he saw her, there was something that took her beautiful to the next level.

"My goodness, you are a beautiful woman," he said taking in all of her.

"Thank you," she responded.

"Wait, I should say hello first, but seeing you I couldn't help myself. You are absolutely stunning and I am one lucky man to be the recipient of your yes to dinner with me tonight," he added.

"I'm going to say that we are both lucky tonight," she said. Secretly, she hoped they would both be getting a lot luckier by the end of the night.

The moment she opened the door and saw Timothy standing on the other side looking scrumptious, all she could think about was the kiss they shared and how good his lips felt. She could only imagine what they would feel like on other parts of her body. Just thinking about it had her tingling all over in anticipation.

She went to move to the side so that he could enter and the moment the door was closed behind them, she felt herself being pulled into his arms and on her gasp of surprise, his luscious mouth came down on hers and she went pliant in his arms, accepting and loving the assault on her mouth. Joining him in the heated exchange, she reached up and held on to his shoulders as he moved her against the back of the door, deepening the kiss. She heard herself moan with delight and when she heard his groans of pleasure, she pulled his shoulders closer to her so that she could feel even more of him. She felt his hands as they came down to encircle her waist, holding her in place while they tried to devour each other. No way was a kiss supposed to feel this wonderful, she thought. Everything about it had her screaming loudly in her head, begging for more and more.

Timothy wondered where the cloud they were floating on had come from. The kiss they were sharing was delicate and enchanting and soon, he would be ready to dispense with dinner and go instead, in search of a bed. Holly was mating with his mouth like she wanted more and he was more than ready for more. He knew from the moment they met that more was in store for them.

Knowing that he needed to slow things down and that they would have time for this and more later, he pulled back as he watched her try to catch her breath like him.

"That's the kind of hello a woman wants every single time," Holly admitted.

"Well, baby, I am to please. Let's make our way to dinner because as good as you look in this dress, I'm losing my appetite for food," he said looking at her from bottom to top.

"Whew. I won't tell you the thoughts that are crossing my mind and if we don't leave for dinner now, I'm not sure I'm letting you out of this house tonight."

Timothy smiled, loving that they were on the same page.

"The way I want you, the way I've wanted you since we met, I'm not sure I'd want to leave this house tonight, but I promised you dinner and dinner is what we'll do. Perhaps we can control ourselves long enough to also do a movie," he added.

Holly moved around him to go in search of her bag and coat.

"We need to do something before we burst into flames together," she laughed.

"This thing between us is powerful. Can you feel it?" he asked softly, leaning down to place a soft kiss on her lips.

"I can and I welcome it. This is really crazy considering we just met earlier this week, but I feel like it's meant to be."

"I feel the same way."

Holly was about to say something else and her stomach growled and they both broke out in a fit of laughter.

"I guess, I need to feed you first," Timothy said.

"Yeah, let's do that," Holly said as they left.

6

Dinner was everything and then some, Holly thought as they shared a lemon soufflé dessert dish. Timothy had taken her to one of the finest restaurants in Chicago where they dined on fresh fish, steamed vegetables and three-times baked potatoes with seafood stuffing that was to die for. He shared with her that a friend of his owned the restaurant which accounted for the private dining area they sat in where they were the only guests.

To her, this was the most magical night of her life. Candles were lit throughout the room and soft music played through speakers that were placed on all sides of the room. Before dinner arrived, they danced and the moment he pulled her into his arms and swayed with her to the music, she got the confirmation she needed that they were meant to be together.

Timothy was everything a woman could want in a man. He was attentive, complimentary and most of all, he was a gentleman taking great care that she was having a fantastic time.

After dinner, they talked and sipped on wine until the dessert came. Now they were enjoying learning even more about each other, dragging out their time together. It was clear neither of them were ready for the night to end.

Timothy looked across at the woman who was changing his outlook on life. It was normally around this time of year when he spent a lot of quiet time alone, not wanting to be around anyone, but this year, he was glad he had Holly to share his time with. Being around her was magical and enticing beyond anything he could have comprehended under any other circumstance. He had entertained female friends before, but Holly was different. In her, he could see forever and a new love for the holiday season. She was showing him how to appreciate every day of every year, including holiday time. Her name alone was enough to brighten his life. The night had been perfect so far and he wanted it to continue.

"Now that dinner is over, I don't want my time with you to end tonight," he said. He knew that Holly was thinking the same thing or he wouldn't have broached the subject. That's the kind of night they were having.

"Neither do I. I'm enjoying being with you very much and I don't want the night to end yet either."

"Well, as I mentioned earlier, I wanted to see if you would like to go take in a movie after dinner, but I don't want to share you with anyone else tonight, not even a bunch of strangers at a theater. Would you like to join me at my place for some after dinner coffee and a movie? We could also grab a few movies and go back to your house if that would make you feel more comfortable as long as I'm not being too forward. I know ladies like to be in their own surroundings and I want this night to be all about you and what you want to do," he added.

Holly didn't hesitate. It didn't matter to her one way or

the other as long as they were together.

"Either works for me. As long as I get to spend more time with you tonight, I don't care what we do as long as we do it together," she said, leaving the ball in his court.

Timothy was grateful that their paths had crossed. He couldn't ask for a more perfect and incredibly beautiful woman who was just as interested in him as he was in her.

"Okay, let's go to my house. We're actually not too far from it."

"I'm ready when you are," she said.

Timothy signaled for the check and when the waiter came over, he informed him that the dinner was comped by the owner. He had to admit that though he didn't have a family to call his own, he had the best friends a guy could ask for that treated him like family.

The owner, Terrence, was someone he'd sold a house to in the past and they'd been good friends since, playing pickup basketball games and doing charity work. Terrence and his wife had been trying to have a baby for over a year and many times, he had confided in Timothy the struggles they'd gone through. Being a friend was just as important as having a friend and he appreciated the friendship they had.

"Thanks for letting me know and tell Terrence, I said thanks and I'll be in touch next week," he said standing to help Holly with her coat.

As they walked outside to the valet to wait for the car, Timothy pulled her close to protect her from the cold, brisk night.

"Are you warm enough? You can wait inside until the car comes, if you like," he said.

Holly looked up at him and felt nothing but warmth.

"I'm as warm as any woman can be with you holding her close. I'm fine right here with you," she admitted, moving in even closer when he pulled her closer into his embrace.

Timothy placed a soft kiss on her cheek just as the car was brought to the curb. He helped her in before providing the valet with a large tip before he got in himself.

"Are you sure you're okay with skipping the theater and going back to my house?"

He knew what the night could be for them and though he would never push her into anything, he wanted her with a fierceness he couldn't explain, but they had to be on the same page.

Holly leaned over and planted a soft, yet intoxicating kiss on his lips to show him that she was right where he was. When she pulled back, if the kiss didn't answer his question, she knew the look in her eyes would. She wanted him just as much as he wanted her.

"Is that answer enough for you?" she asked.

"More than you could know," he said, pulling out into traffic.

Holly was excited and glad that she'd thought to pack a small necessity bag just in case that was small enough to fit in her purse. Whatever the night held for them, she was open and ready for. She knew that from the moment she'd first laid eyes on him.

~~

So that he didn't appear too anxious to divest Holly of all of her clothes, Timothy got the movie started when they reached his house and then went in search of some wine and snacks for them to enjoy. He wanted her naked, but he also wanted to have time to just sit and enjoy being together.

When he returned, he was happy to see that Holly had already made herself more comfortable. She had taken off her high heeled shoes and stockings and was sitting with her legs tucked under her looking relaxed. He told her to get as comfortable as she liked. When they first arrived, he had given her a quick tour of his place and then showed her his media room where they could sit back and relax and he'd even let her pick the movie from his large selection.

Walking into the room, he joined her on the double recliner as the opening credits completed rolling and poured them each a glass of wine while he placed the tray filled with fruit, cheeses and meats within arm's reach of them. He settled in next to her and pulled her closer to him so that they could snuggle.

"This feels right," he whispered to her.

"It feels wonderful. I'm glad you thought of it. This is how I'd like to always unwind after a long work week."

"Well, you can come and unwind with me anytime you want. You're always welcomed."

Holly looked away from the movie and looked up into Timothy's face. This is the man I've been waiting a lifetime for, she thought. This man right here was turning into everything she'd the man of her dreams would be. The dinner really sealed things for her as they talked, danced and ate while learning even more about each other. The intense connection they'd shared from the moment they met was still there and had not diminished any. She was ready for more and from the look in Timothy's eyes, so was he.

No longer were words needed and no longer did the television screen interest either one of them.

"Will you stay the night with me tonight?" he asked.

Maybe he was going too fast and needed to back off, but the pull to her was too great to be ignored.

When Holly smiled, he knew they were together in their thoughts.

"I thought you'd never ask," she said before turning further into his arms. Holly saw the look in his eyes that she'd seen earlier in the night when he consumed her with a burning kiss.

Again, she didn't have to wait long for the next one either. The kiss seemed natural as if they'd been doing it for years together. They naturally moved in sync with each other, already knowing what they both wanted and needed and right now, they needed each other. Frustration settled in when she couldn't get any closer to Timothy due to the constraints of the chair.

Timothy couldn't seem to get enough and from the reaction he was getting from Holly, neither was she. On any other day, he loved the chairs in his media room, but for what he had in mind, today it was a hindrance. He had a remedy as he reached for her, lifting her from the chair, still kissing her deeply, not wanting to break the connection.

Holly felt herself being lifted and cheered inwardly that they always seem to be on the same page. She went willingly when Timothy picked her up and headed for the steps that she assumed lead to his bedroom. At this point, she would settle for any room with a bed.

When Timothy reached his room, he hesitated only for a second to turn on a soft light so that they could see each other. If he was going to get her naked, he didn't want to miss any chance at getting a good look at the gorgeous body he'd been imagining all evening.

He moved further toward the bed with her still in his arms and her legs wrapped tightly around his waist. Timothy had no doubt Holly could feel how much he desired her as his hard length grew longer and harder than he could ever imagine it being in the past. He had no doubt only Holly could get him to his current state of arousal.

Pulling back from the kiss, Timothy looked into her glazed over eyes and knew that the heated exchange between them was just the beginning, but he needed to make sure he wasn't moving them too fast.

"Are you sure about this he asked? As much as I want you, I have no problem taking a quick ice cold shower and returning to the movie we were preparing to act like we were watching," he said, adding humor.

There was no doubt in Holly's mind that what they were about to do was in the stars for them the moment they met and she wasn't about to deny either of them.

"I want you just as much, if not more and I'm about to have a real problem if you make me wait any longer," she said in a sexy, husky voice she never knew she had. That was a testament to how paramount her need for him was.

Not needing any coaxing, Timothy turned so that he sat down on the edge of his bed with Holly straddling his lap. He slid her dress high up over her hips so that he could caress her lush round behind. His need for her went up a notch when his hands didn't encounter panties, but instead, his fingers caressed the very thin line of her thong that rested between her cheeks.

The thought that he'd sat across from her all evening and all she had on underneath was this thin strap of material was a major turn-on. Needing to feel more of her, he reached around and slid the arms of her dress down where his eyes feasted on the sheer navy blue lace of her demi-cup bra.

"You are so beautiful," he said.

Holly was about to respond when her words got caught in her throat as Timothy leaned forward, snaked his tongue out and licked across the hard nub of first one nipple and then the other and an erotic surge went through her straight to that area between her legs that yearned for him the most. She moaned her delight and held on to his shoulders to be sure she stayed seated on his lap on top of the hard ridge of his erection that provided her with an early feel of him against her sensitive mound.

Timothy sucked her through her bra before sliding the cups down and taking a full nipple into his mouth, pulling and caressing it with suction that elicited more sounds of pleasure from Holly. He knew that she had no idea that her sounds were driving him wild for her.

"You like that," he said, loving her reaction to him.

"I love it. Give me more," Holly said without shame.

"I'll give you whatever you want," he uttered.

He then reached down for the hem of her dress and pulled it up and over her head until it was completely off. That left her sitting in his lap in nothing but her bra and a matching thong he wasn't sure was actually there it was so stringy and sexy. He wasted no time removing the bra and as soon as he noticed the ties on each side of her hip that held her thong in place, he pulled the strings and that fell away as well. Holly sat astride him completely naked and he was the happiest and horniest he has ever been before.

"I like you just like this Holly," he said catching the sinful look of desire that stared back at him.

"I like you like this," she said, at the same time, grinding on him mercilessly, letting him know exactly what she wanted.

He saw no reason to make either of them wait any longer. He stood up, turned around and after placing her in the center of his bed, he quickly divested himself of all of his clothing and reached into his nightstand to withdraw the protection they would need. He then joined her on the bed, moving over her as he leaned down and planted soft kisses all over her body. He continued his ministrations even as Holly squirmed around underneath of him. He wanted to be sure she was as ready for him as he was for her.

Moving up so that they were looking in each other's eyes, he held her stare as he quickly donned the condom. In a swift motion, he slid between her legs, rolled so that she was on top and without much effort, he lifted her body up so that he could slide her ever so slowly back down on him in one slow and steady plunge. Before he could set the pace, Holly began grinding, not just up and down on him, but around and around showing him how she liked it. He too was on board for that. Just when he thought he was about to rock her world, she turned the tables and he was already close to his release.

"Oh, what are you doing to me baby," he crooned like a starving man as he leaned into her chest to try and absorb her body right into his, never wanting to let her go.

"I'm showing you how much I've wanted you since the second we met," Holly admitted while increasing the pace of her downward thrusts.

Then the only sound heard in the room were the slippery, wet sounds of his body entering hers over and over again as she rocked on top of him. The sound was the most erotic sound Timothy had ever heard and he knew he was about to lose it, but didn't want to do so without her.

He reached down to the area where his body was joined with hers and using his fingers, he stroked her hardened nub on each pass up his hard flesh. When her small cries grew louder, he knew she was on the edge, right where he wanted her to be.

Holly felt her orgasm rising as she quickened the pace of her movements, loving the feel of Timothy pushing up to meet her downward thrusts. They were together and together they would soar into an erotic zone where nothing existed but them and the feelings they were pulling from each other. She held on to his shoulders as she arched her back and rode him like a starving woman.

"I'm almost there," she moaned, letting him know of her pending release.

"That's right baby. I want you to let go and I want us to do this together because I'm right there with you. Now Holly," Timothy shouted and the air around them crackled as they came together in a heated blaze that rocked them both to their core.

As her release gripped her, Holly felt rockets shooting off in her body. She was on a higher plateau than she'd ever experienced before and she never wanted to come down.

"That's it baby. Let go," Timothy crooned in her ear as she leaned down riding out the last semblance of her powerful release.

As Holly soared, Timothy climbed with her as his body crashed over and over again. His orgasm was so strong, he had to grit his teeth due to the magnitude of the zings flowing through his body, starting first at his feet and sliding throughout all parts of his body. He held onto Holly's waste as tight as he could without leaving a mark and he pumped relentlessly into her body, embracing his own powerful release as it fired up again and again and then yet again.

His screams of pleasure were mixed with her screams of joy as they together enjoyed the perfect moment together. A moment neither ever wanted to be without again.

7

"Do you realize I have been dating Timothy for two whole weeks and I swear I have never, ever been happier in my life," Holly told Teresa as she walked around her room trying to get dressed knowing that Timothy was on his way over. Teresa called just as she had gotten out of the shower.

"I'm liking this guy more and more because I agree, you have never been this happy in a relationship. There must be something special about him because you've kept him locked away under lock and key since you met. I cannot believe I haven't met mister wonderful yet. Speaking of that, when will I be meeting him? I know you've told him something about me by now and he's anxious to meet the one woman you consider closer than any sister could ever be," Teresa said facetiously.

Holly laughed out loud.

"I hear you and I was planning on asking him about meeting you for dinner one day this week. You know Christmas is coming up and I have a lot planned for the kids at the home so I want to get the dinner in before I get extremely busy. How does that work?"

"That works for me. I can't wait to grill him on all the questions a sister I supposed to ask the man who has kept you tied to a bed for the past two weeks."

"How do you know I haven't kept him tied to a bed?" Holly asked.

"You're right. I have to remember the wild seductress you are and he'll probably be glad to get out and having dinner so that his body can get a rest."

"Whew, I tell you that man is something else, in and out of the bed. He's not only a great guy, but he does wonderful things in the community and you know how I feel about that. I want to say we are perfect together, but I don't want to sound vain."

"Girl, claim that relationship in any way you want because you deserve to be this happy and to have a man who makes you this happy. I can't wait to meet him. I'm going to let you go because I know you're preparing for your man. I wanted to call and check in since I haven't heard from you. Let that man up for air sometime and call me," Teresa laughed.

"Yeah, yeah. I'll call you later," Holly said before hanging up and rushing to get dressed.

Two and a half weeks and the relationship with Timothy was going full steam. No one could have told her that walking into the real estate office would introduce her to the man of her dreams.

Over the past few weeks, they spent a lot of time together, both professional and personal. She decided on the house she wanted to purchase for the kids and he moved swiftly to get everything in place so that the kids would have a bigger and nicer place to call home until a more permanent family came calling for them. When they weren't dealing with issues around the purchase, they were going dancing, checking out other restaurants around town and taking in a concert. She was having the time of her life and while doing so, falling in love. Timothy made it easy for her to get the kind of feelings for him that she'd never had for another man before. Tonight, they were going to enjoy a night at her house and after the busy day she'd had, she couldn't wait to relax with him. Connecting with him had become the highlight of her day and each day kept getting better and better.

~~

Timothy walked up to Holly's house ready for a nice, quiet evening. He smiled remembering how good the last couple of weeks with her had been. They had spent just about every evening together, whether at his house or hers and had fallen into a routine that was as natural as breathing.

Ringing the doorbell, his heart swelled when Holly opened the door to him with his arms loaded with and a smile on her face that lit up the room. This was his woman, he thought. This beautiful, gorgeous, vivacious woman was his. Tonight, they were going to chill mix in a little work to go over the final details about the house.

Everything with the purchase went smooth and quick. Now that his part in her process was over, he was helping her with the move-in timeframe and the purchase of new furniture. He, himself along with a few of his other friends who owned businesses and looked for opportunities to give back, would be donating all of the computers and other equipment like printers and software for the new computer lab. He was excited to be a part of the project of helping the kids have a better life while they lived at the home.

"Hey beautiful," he said leaning over to plant one of his fiery kisses on her. His mind had been on her delicious lips all day.

"Hi, baby," Holly replied returning the kiss that she desperately needed. She wasn't having a good day and tried hard to plaster a smile on her face in order to not have her bad day impact their evening together.

Timothy noticed something was off. He had grown to know her well, making sure he took note of anything that took her radiant smile away. He could see they needed to talk because nothing brought him greater joy than to see Holly happy.

As Holly locked the door, he made his way into the kitchen where he proceeded to lay out the food and look for eating utensils.

"What's gotten you down today?" he asked.

Holly followed him and leaned against the counter to watch him work. She was one lucky woman to have such and incredibly handsome man who was open about taking care of her and caring about what she was going through both good and bad.

"I was supposed to have a pool party tomorrow for the kids at the local YWCA. Today they had a major pipe burst at the facility and it will be closed until after the Christmas holiday. I was hoping to have the party to cheer some of them up who were feeling a little down as we are getting closer to Christmas. Now, I have to tell them tomorrow that we have to wait until after we move in the New Year to have the party. They were really looking forward to it," she said sadly.

Timothy had a solution without a second guess.

"You still can," he said.

"How?" she asked.

"You can have it at my house. You know I have an indoor pool and I do have a busy Saturday this weekend so you are more than welcomed to bring the kids over for the party on Saturday and I won't be in your hair. I can have a caterer brought in to prepared some grilled burgers and hotdogs with all the fixings and trimmings. Let's see, all we would need to do would be to hire some lifeguards to watch the kids while they're in the pool. I'm sure we could check with some of the one's who work at the YWCA. Since it's closed, I'm sure those who were looking forward to that money for holiday shopping wouldn't mind making some extra money and my company can foot the bill for that. I have a friend who owns a restaurant that I can get to do the food. We can order a cake and some balloons and let them have a real party. You can use the bus you have at the home to bring the kids and I'm sure they would have a blast. What do you think?" he asked. He knew he would do anything to fix the sad look he saw on her face even if she tried to mask it with a smile.

Holly didn't say anything. She came around the marble island in her kitchen and leaped into his arms. She plastered kisses all across his face while repeating words of thanks.

"You are amazing, Timothy. I am one lucky woman. Are you sure you don't mind? I don't want them messing up your gorgeous house."

"I don't mind at all and I would do anything for you within my power and that my lady, is within my power. So, is it settled?" he asked.

"Yes, it is and thank you baby. I love you for that," Holly said, not afraid that she'd just told him she loved him. It wasn't a problem for her because she did. Perhaps it was too soon, she thought, to say the word love, but it was how she felt. They had grown closer since they first began dating and love had blossomed as it should when two people have the kind of connection they shared. It was love at first sight and that love had grown with each passing moment.

Timothy heard her say love and where most men may be hesitant at hearing those words after only a few weeks of dating, he embraced it just as he embraced her in his arms.

"I love you too, baby. I love you very much," he said before pulling her further up in his arms, wrapping her legs around his back and bringing her in for a much better kiss than the one he gave her when he came in the door.

"Why don't we put this food away until a little later. I have something in mind for right now," she said.

Timothy knew that look and knew what it meant. His woman needed him and since there was never a time when he didn't need her, he kissed her sweetly and deeply, letting her know he was ready to provide anything she wanted and needed at any time, including right now.

"I say we leave the food right where it is because I don't plan to put you down until I reach a bed," Timothy said, doing just that. He moved swiftly toward the steps that led to her bedroom to make love to the woman who had come to be his everything. That's saying a lot for a man who spent years around this time of year hating everything about it. Now, all he knew was love and that love gave him a new outlook on the holiday and life in general.

8

Timothy came home just as the pool party at his house was wrapping up. After Holly arrived at his house early in the day with a decorator to get ready for the kids to have their pool party, he gave her the key and told her to do whatever she wanted. He had a lot of work to do and he left with an extra pep in his step knowing he'd put a huge smile on the face of the woman who had completely changed his life.

For the first time in his life, he was excited about the holiday season, especially Christmas. Someone telling him he wouldn't be a bah humbug again this year would have been lost on him if he wasn't living the change himself. He owed a lot of what he was feeling to Holly. She showed him what real, true love was all about, not just with him being open to receiving love, but giving it over freely.

After entering his house, he headed toward the back of his house where his indoor pool was located. Before he reached the room, he could hear the chatter and laughter of the kids and he loved it. This is what he would have loved to have back when he lived in a group home. It brought him joy to be able to provide this for them.

He looked around and the kids looked like they'd had a great time. He knew when he decided to build this house that he wanted a huge indoor pool since he loved to swim and with the cold weather being a constant in Chicago, he wanted to be able to swim all year.

He saw the three lifeguards that had been hired for the day and caught them assisting with the cleanup as well. He'd had to make sure he gave them an extra tip for going above and beyond. The food was a big hit as well as he took in remnants of hotdogs, chicken, burgers, chips, salads, juices, desserts and tons of fixings for everything. Nothing brought him as much joy when it came to kids as this very moment. He was about to turn around and head to the part of his house where his bedroom was to shower and change when Holly noticed him. He was hoping to get a glimpse, but to remain out of the way. There were over twenty volunteers helping her with the kids and he didn't need to be in the way. He smiled at her when she asked him to come over so that the kids could thank him for the use of his house.

After introducing him, he was overwhelmed with love when the kids came running over to thank him, telling him about the great time they'd had.

"I'm glad you all enjoyed yourselves," he said.

"Yeah!" the kids screamed together.

"Go on back and have a little more fun before you leave," he told them.

The kids ran off except for one little girl who had her body glued to Holly, gripping onto Holly's legs as if she was afraid to let go. His first thought when he saw the little girl was how anyone could abandon such a sweet child. All of the children at the home were without parents and because he knew what that felt like, he felt sorry for them. All children deserved to be loved and have a family that wants and loves them. When she smiled up at him after placing her thumb in her mouth, he knelt down to be on her level.

"Don't you want to go play a little more as well?" he asked her.

She nodded her head yes, never taking her finger out of her mouth. Before he knew what was happening, she had grabbed him around the neck in a vice-like hug.

"Thank you for letting me swim in your pool. I love to swim and I had fun. I also ate a hotdog, which is my favorite after pizza."

Timothy patted her on the head, overwhelmed with emotion. This is what life was about, he thought. Bringing a smile, fun and laughter into the life of a child should be a goal of every adult's life.

"You are welcomed sweetheart. What's your name?" he asked.

"Angel," she replied.

"Wow, what a beautiful name you have and it's a special one because you certainly are a little angel with a big hug and smile like that. I'm glad you had a good time," he said.

Holly watched the exchange and knew that it meant just as much to Timothy as it had to Angel. During their many talks, he'd told her that he grew up having a hard time expressing himself and relating to people. Watching his exchange with Angel warmed her heart.

"Okay, Angel, go gather your things together and you have a few more minutes to play before we leave soon so that everyone can go home, get baths and watch a movie before bed," Holly said. She smiled when angel nodded her head and ran off behind the other children.

"What a lovely child," Timothy acknowledged.

"I agree and one day when I have children, I want a little girl just like her. I don't want to just have my own children, but I also want to adopt children like her who are waiting for the right family to embrace them. Even though people often look to birth all of their children, I believe that there are lots of children who are already here who could use loving homes."

Timothy loved Holly's kind, open heart. It's one of the many things he loved about her. He reached out and pulled her back into his embrace. He was overwhelmed with how much he loved her.

"I'm sure you will," is all he said. He knew that she wasn't making a play for marriage and babies with him, but it's what he was thinking. He wanted to be the man to give her the world including all the children she wanted to have through birth and adoption. This wasn't the moment to address it, but he held the thought in his mind for the perfect opportunity to bring it up again. He kissed her on the cheek.

"Look at how happy they are," she said.

"I see their happiness and it looks a lot like yours."

"This is all because of you. I love you," she said.

Kissing her one last time, he knew it was time to remove himself as a distraction.

"I love you, too and I'm going to go grab a shower so that I can come back to help get everyone together and on the bus. I'll have the caterer prepare the extra food to take back with you so that the kids can have it later on. That way, you won't have to cook."

"You think of everything," she said.

"As long as you're happy, I'm happy."

"We need to clean up first," she said looking around.

"Nonsense. I have a crew coming in about an hour that will have this place looking like its brand new. Just leave everything for them and focus on the kids. Make sure the kids don't leave anything behind so that it doesn't get tossed away," he said.

"You are the best," Holly said with pure joy.

"I'll be right back," he said walking off.

~~

"The children had a wonderful time at your house today. I don't think I could ever thank you enough for allowing us to be here. I hope we didn't make too much of a mess," Holly said as she walked back into the house behind Timothy.

He helped her and her team of volunteers and staff at the children's home get the kids on the bus to go back home. Most were already sleep before the bus pulled out of his driveway.

"My house is your house," he said, meaning every word of it.

"You are so wonderful to me," she said sweetly.

"Are you sure you don't have to leave to help with the children?" he asked when they reached the kitchen and he took out a bottle of wine for them to enjoy while they relaxed.

"I'm sure. Those are the staff members who work there around the clock and they'll do well with getting the children settled. I try not to let the children think I'll be there all the time since I don't live on the premises. The kids need to depend on the staff for things though I do make myself available when needed. I already have a hard time getting Angel to realize I won't be at the house all the time. The staff tells me she asks for me often and that's due to the fact that we have developed quite a connection. She's so young and would make a great addition to any home. I can't believe it has taken a long time to find a family for her. She is the sweetest, most delicate and charming little girl I've ever met."

Timothy watched Holly as she talked about Angel. He could tell that deep down, she wished Angel could be hers. He could see them together doing fun mother and daughter things. If nothing else, Holly is going to one day be a wonderful mother.

"You know I will never, ever tire of having you around. I just want to be sure I'm not keeping you from anything, especially the children. I don't want to get excited about having you to myself all night only to find you need to leave. You know I'd understand, but what can I say, I am selfish when it comes to you," he said leaning down for a delectable kiss.

"I'm all yours," Holly said tenderly.

"Mmm," he moaned when he realized they needed to be someplace else other than in the kitchen for what he had in mind.

"Mmm, is right," she added.

"I think it's time we retired to another part of the house. No need in giving the cleaning crew a show since they'll be coming back and forth to the kitchen to finish up."

"I'm right with you, babe. I'm feeling rather frisky tonight and I have some things I want to show you," Holly said.

"Then why are we still standing here," he said as he walked off toward the part of the house that held his private bedroom quarters.

When they reached the bedroom, Holly entered first as Timothy followed her and locked the door behind him. Thankfully, his housekeeper was at the house to see to the final cleanup and he could focus all of his attention on Holly and their desirous need for each other.

Timothy reached for Holly and she moved into his embrace until their bodies were flush against each other.

"You are everything to me," he said.

"That sentiment is mutual," Holly swooned as she leaned up to get a little closer to his lips.

Not making her wait, Timothy kissed her plump lips, teasing them first with his tongue, tracing the seam from one side to the other. When she moaned out loud, he intensified the connection, but enticing her to open her lips for him. Going in like a starving man, a shiver rippled through him as the kiss turned hotter and hotter. Their breathing became erratic as he reached down and searched for the hem of her blouse. Pulling it up and over her head, he leaned down and pressed soft kisses along the sleek line of her neck. Timothy caressed her bare back as he unsnapped the clasp of her bra and smiled as it fell away, giving him access to her large round globes.

Sliding down her body, he could feel her legs begin to shake when she reached out to brace herself by grasping his shoulders. He sucked one nipple into his mouth, giving it extra attention before moving over to give the same attention to the other.

Holly's skin was on fire as her one and only focus became how good Timothy was making her feel. He never failed to elicit a pleasure beyond belief from her, causing a fire to burn inside of her that could only be doused by him.

"More," she uttered as she through her head back,

enjoying the spikes of pleasure that ricocheted from her breasts where his tongue delighted her, all the way through other pleasure points across her body.

Timothy gave her more when he slid her skirt and panties down her legs together. He moaned when her scent overpowered him as his nose came in direct contact with the apex of her thighs. He could smell how aroused she was and it caused his body to harden.

"You smell delicious and I can't wait to taste you," he said.

Holly tried to respond when her words got lost in the feeling of his tongue sliding against her already moist center. She tried to move her legs to open them a little more for him to get even better access, but couldn't as she felt like she was going to collapse any moment from the climax that was already flowing through her body.

"Yes," she squealed when Timothy lapped at her, focusing on her hard nub. Without warning, her body exploded when he mixed sucking on her nub to blowing a whisper of breath on her, sending her over the edge. Her lips moved on their own accord as she rode out her climax. Only when her body started to calm did she fall like a heap of clay into his arms.

"I needed that as much as you," Timothy said as he lifted her from the floor where they stood and placed her on his bed.

Quickly removing his clothes, he kept his eyes on the woman he loved, taking in the heat of her gaze as she stretched and waited for him to join her.

Making quick work of tossing his clothes to the floor, he moved to the nightstand to retrieve a condom and almost lost sight of what he was doing when Holly reached out to grip the steely length of his hardness in her hand and began stroking him. Timothy didn't think he could get any harder, but with Holly, it was possible. He hissed out his pleasure as he struggled to get the condom package open.

"I love how hard and powerfully strong you get, especially when I grip you like this," she said continuing to stroke his hardness from base to tip.

"I love how soft your hand is around my hardness, but if I don't soon get inside of you, I think I'm going to go mad," he said through gritted teeth.

Holly smiled at the reaction she received and giggled when Timothy finally joined her on the bed, grabbing her to kiss her passionately as he did his best to roll on protection.

"I'm ready when you are," she said, saucily.

Timothy didn't need any more of an invitation as he moved so that he was in between her silky, soft legs and as he leaned down for a passionate kiss, sliding his tongue in deep while he slid into her body with one long, powerful surge forward, taking their breath away. He wasted no time gliding in and out, slowly at first until the grind of Holly's hips caused him to increase his thrusts. A throaty moan escaped his mouth as he stroked in deep before pulling out to go back in again. The feeling was immeasurable the moment Holly gripped him with her inner muscles. He inhaled and held it as his mind reeled from the magnitude of what his body was going through.

"I feel you baby. Are you with me?" he asked, barely able to hold on, but he would until she was with him.

"I'm here baby and I'm with you," Holly said. She leaned her face into his chest as her climax took over her body completely while her hips pumped up while Timothy pumped down into her wildly.

Feeling her explode, Timothy let go as his body edged toward a cliff and spasms consumed him. When Holly tilted her hips slightly, his orgasm was prolonged as a soul-stirring moan escaped while rockets shot off in his head.

They remained in the throes of ecstasy until together, they calmed and held on to each other, neither wanting to move.

Holly knew this was a moment she always wanted to share with Timothy. There was so much love involved in their coming together that she knew she would be empty without it; without him.

"I love you," Timothy said, moving from her body to the side of her, pulling her along with him so that he could cradle her in his arms.

"I love you," Holly whispered before getting as close to him as she could as sleep overtook her. Her last memory was of Timothy pulling the blanket up and over them and whispering over and over how much he loved her. She also remembered hearing him thank her for making him a new man. What he didn't know was that it meant just as much to her as it did to him.

9

"Do you know I've never really celebrated Christmas before?" Timothy said to Holly as she moved about the kitchen gathering items to make breakfast. They were both starving after working up an appetite the night before and well into the morning.

"Never? I know you told me that it wasn't your favorite holiday, but you never said you didn't celebrate it," she said.

"Well, when I was young, the group home always had gifts for us and a Santa Claus would always come through. Other people would also stop by with gifts for us, but nothing like what I heard other kids at school talking about who had mothers and fathers. Even the years I spent with different foster families was okay, but never really felt like Christmas to me. It never measured up to what I thought it was supposed to be, you know with a mother and a father, sisters and brothers getting together on Christmas morning to open gifts, sing songs and all those fun things. You watch different Christmas movies that show what it's supposed to be like and that just never happened for me. Only because of you is there a huge tree in my living room

84

right now."

Prior to having the kids over for their pool party, he made sure he had the house decorated for Christmas with the largest Christmas tree he could find. He had to have everything brought new because he didn't own any kind of decorations.

"That's a sad story, but I'm glad it has turned into a happy one."

"I agree," Timothy said kissing her on the lips before going back to helping her prepare breakfast. He'd given his housekeeper the day off so that he could spend the morning with Holly alone.

"I intend to make sure this is the best Christmas that you could possibly have."

"You're already doing that, which is why I love you. Other than having Christmas as a young child, as an adult, I've never even thought to purchase a tree to decorate let alone all of the other decorations. I told my housekeeper to make the house look like Christmas and I had no idea she would do it in every room of the house. I guess she said as long as I gave her the power to do as she saw fit, she went overboard, but I admit, I love it. See how much of an impact you've had on my life? No one would believe I just said I love these decorations," Timothy said with so much love and affection for her.

"Our lives as children were not much different Timothy. I vowed that one day I would do whatever I could to help kids get adopted, so that those times that I felt helpless or that no one truly loved me would never be how another child who crossed my path would feel. Because of you and how big your heart is, the kids had a great time and they loved your tree and the decorations."

Timothy went over to Holly to pull her into a tight embrace.

"You have such a huge heart. I love that about you. When I told you I loved you, I never thought I'd ever say that to anyone. I'm not sure I ever really knew what the feeling of love was because other than my best friend and his wife who have always shown me love, I didn't have much to go by to know what it was like to feel love and to be loved. I've always been close to friends and they've embraced me in their lives, but to actually have the feeling that my life would be even emptier without someone is how I feel right now. I'm not afraid to embrace being in love with you and looking forward to where that love will take us. This is the best Christmas season ever!" he said.

"I love you too, Timothy. This thing between us has been a whirlwind and I wouldn't change a thing," she said.

"Neither would I love. You know, I've been thinking a lot about our discussion the other night about how we can help the children at the Open Care House and I have an idea. It's an idea inspired by how kindhearted you are."

Holly moved to sit across from him at the island as they ate.

"Okay, let's hear it," she said, intrigued.

"I've been reaching out to some contacts who are attorneys around Chicago and a few in the New York area, too. They work with families who are looking to adopt. Most have already completed the necessary paperwork and I thought it would be a great idea to bring the families together with the children at the home to see if we can get some of the children into some good homes. Now each of them say the parents have been thoroughly screened, so we don't have to wait for that process to complete and according to my contacts, these are some pretty great families, all of whom are excited about the possibility of adopting a child and none are concerned about them being infants like a lot of them are. Their only concern is about providing a happy and loving home for kids in need. I've been getting faxes all week with information on each of them. What I would need from you to make this happen is information on each child, including their biographical information and photos and then I can send the information to the attorneys and let the families take a look at the children. For those interested, I was thinking of hosting a big holiday gala for Christmas and I think we should invite the families to come and have the children there as well. I believe that by the end of the night, each one of those children will have a brand new place to call home. How does that sound?" he asked, looking down at his food to season the delicious looking veggie omelet she prepared.

When he didn't get a response, he looked over at Holly who was crying so hard her body was shaking.

"What did I ever do to deserve a man like you," she said through her cries.

"It's okay, baby. I know how you feel and like I told you before, I would do anything for you. I know what those kids mean to you and because they do, they mean a lot to me too. You have no idea the joy you've brought into my life and you opened up my eyes to what I can do to help them."

"All I can say is thank you. You are one special man. We were brought together not just to find the love we both have been searching for all of our lives, but there was a plan in place for us to put our heads and hearts together to help these children. Having the new children's home is nice, but I'd rather have the house sitting empty because we don't need it, than to continue to have it overflowing with children year after year. I think it's a wonderful idea and I know that the city will think this is a fantastic idea and will be behind it one hundred percent. I'm going to get on it today and get you everything you need. This will be the best Christmas ever for the kids and for me also."

"Sweetie, this has turned out to be the best year of my life and I can't wait to see what the next year has in store for us. Let's finish eating breakfast and then we'll both dig in to see what we can get accomplished by the end of the day," Timothy said.

10

Employees of TRC Realty were all arriving around their normal time for work the week before Christmas. They were used to their boss giving them Christmas Eve and the week between Christmas and New Year's Day off, but they all knew the office would be open and operating on the regular schedule until then. They were excited and expecting to participate in the small office holiday celebration Timothy allowed them to have each year. Nothing seemed out of the ordinary as Ariana, Jeffrey and three other realtors walked up to the office building. The out of ordinary happened when Ariana reached to open the office door and it was locked. For years, Timothy employed security that came by an hour before everyone arrived and unlocked the doors and took a quick check around before taking their position in the main lobby. They were always the first to arrive ahead of the other thirty team members he employed.

Today, the front door to the building was locked and no security guards could be seen at the security desk. Everyone looked at each other strange as if any one of them would have a clue about what was going on.

"This is strange," Ariana said, concerned.

Surely the office isn't closing without a word of warning from their boss, she thought.

"I agree," Jeffrey chimed in. "I've never arrived at work and the doors were still locked."

Everyone agreed.

"Wait, there's a note on the side glass panel," Ariana said, reaching for it then reading it aloud.

"Dear staff, the offices of TRC Realty will be closed for the day."

Ariana stopped reading and looked around at everyone else. She continued reading.

"In recognition of the joyous holiday season, please join me for a company celebration at the Starlight Restaurant. Since today is a Saturday, feel free to bring your mates, spouses and children and Santa Claus will be on hand to celebrate with the children. Merry Christmas to you all. See you at noon, Timothy."

Blank stares greeted Ariana as she looked from one person to the other as other employees of TRC Realty began arriving.

"Ok, who is this guy, Timothy, talking about Merry Christmas and what did he do with our bah humbug boss Timothy?" one of the other staff members said.

"I'm telling you, it's Holly. He hasn't been the same since he met her," Ariana said.

"I agree. The change in him is a refreshing change. It appears he's finally found someone who has shown him what the holiday season is all about. I like this new Timothy," one employee said.

Jeffrey nodded.

"I've actually seen him smile when I tell him she's on the phone for him," Ariana said.

"Well, I don't care what's going on. The office is closed and we're having a big party. I'm going to go home to get my wife and kids together to get to the party on time. Are all of you coming?" Jeffrey asked.

"Yes!" they all chimed in together.

Ariana watched as others walked away as she smiled. She knew something had changed the day Holly Day walked into the office. She had always admired her boss and all of the great things he did for his staff and the community and though he loved making other people happy, she never felt that happiness extended to him. She was happy that his new love interest brought out who he was on the inside.

"Merry Christmas, Mr. Cornish," she said and walked in the direction the others had walked.

~~

Christmas music could be heard coming from the restaurant before anyone entered through the front door. The staff of TRC Realty were shocked when they saw all of the decorations and food being provided for them.

Timothy watched as family after family of his staff arrived. He couldn't wait to share holiday cheer and plans for the New Year with them.

After everyone had taken seats after socializing, Timothy stood to make a toast.

"Thank you all for coming. This year has been an exciting year and I wanted to celebrate that with you and thank you for all that you do. Some of you have been with me from the very beginning and you are the ones who keep coming up to me telling me that you like this new me. I wanted to say thank you for that. I didn't realize until this year that I was that person that everyone wanted to avoid. I admit I made a point of avoiding everyone, but that's all changing. Most of you know that I've met the most incredible woman and fallen in love."

That declaration was met by a round of applause around the tables.

Timothy inwardly cheered himself. It was how he felt every time he thought about Holly.

"Here, here!" someone shouted and they all clapped.

"Thank you all for that. It was because of her that I finally learned to let go of my past and embrace a happy future for myself. That began with her and it now carries over to you. I've said goodbye to the Grinch and so long to that bah humbug person you saw enter the office every day and I've said hello and please to meet you to the Timothy Cornish you see before you today who now embraces the Christmas season. I wanted to take this holiday season and share some time with you all, something I've never done. So, please eat up and when we're done, I think Santa is even going to make an unexpected stop here for the children."

The children shouted with joy. This is what life was about, he thought.

As Timothy sat down, Ariana stood to say a few words.

"Mr. Cornish, we all want to say thank you."

"We're not in the office, so please call me Timothy," he said interrupting her.

"Timothy, TRC is a wonderful place to work whether it was the Grinch or the new and improved Timothy. We all care about you a great deal. We also know what your life was like years ago, so we understood. You've shared your life and history with us and we're glad things have turned around for you. We're just happy that you recognized that your past does not have to define you or follow you around like a crutch. We'll always be here for you. We also want to offer our help with the event you and Holly are having to pair up children at the Open Care House with families who are looking to adopt. We all plan to attend and whatever you need us to do to help, just let us know," she said before taking her seat. Everyone else around the room agreed and clapped to show their support.

Timothy had shared with his staff his plans for the children and he had no doubt they would all want to be a part.

"Thanks to each of you. Holly and I could certainly use your help. Why don't you all join others who are volunteering as well, at my house tomorrow night for the final meeting. I can tell you right now that this event will be the talk of Chicago by the end of the night. It's going to be major. More clapping ensued as bowls and baskets of food were passed around the table.

Timothy sat back and looked around the table. No more avoiding people around the holiday and from this day on, no matter what happened between him and Holly, the holiday was meant to spread love, be loved and be loving and he was going to embrace each of them.

~~

Timothy was following Holly around placing gift wrapped boxes under the huge Christmas tree at the holiday adoption gala. It was Timothy's idea to have a large tree, bigger than the one she was originally planning on putting up at the elegantly decorated hall. They knew they were having lots of guests and most of those guests were the kids at the Open Care House children's home and they wanted to be sure each child left with more than just one gift. Timothy and Holly were ecstatic to see that so many people had caring hearts and donated more gifts and toys than they ever dreamed of. There were dolls, bikes, board games and electronic devices for kids of all ages.

"I'm going to check on the children one more time," Holly said nervously reaching for her cell phone. Timothy grabbed it out of her hands before she could dial.

"Stop worrying, baby. They will be here soon and I trust Saul. I gave him specific instructions on what time to pick up the kids and what time to have them and your staff here. Stop worrying," he said.

Saul was a friend of his who owned a limousine service and he was happy when Saul volunteered to drive the kids and staff to the event in limousines. The kids had never been in any kind of expensive vehicle. He was excited about putting a smile on their little faces.

"I know you're right. I'm just so excited about today. I hope everything turns out right. You did check all of the RSVPs again didn't you?" she asked.

"I checked them many times and everyone we sent information and invitations to have replied that they are excited about coming. The idea of families looking to adopt children from the group home was a fantastic idea," Timothy said.

Holly was about to respond and worry more when they looked up to see that the children had finally arrived. The excitement on their faces was priceless as the evening was about to finally start.

The kids came running to her to get hugs before turning their attention to the tree and the many gifts under it.

"They look so beautiful," Holly said.

She didn't think her day could get any better a few days ago, when one of the largest clothing stores in Chicago showed up, offering to provide new clothing for the kids for the event for free, thanks to Timothy's request. The little girls had their hair done with ribbons and bows, dressed in holiday colored dresses while the boys had fresh haircuts and suits with bowties. Her heart swelled with love.

"Yes, they do and so do you. Go ahead and run over to them. I know you want to," he laughed.

Holly laughed, too.

"You're right. I'll see you in a bit," she said before kissing him sweetly and joining the kids at the tree.

Two hours later, Timothy stood at the podium to speak.

"Hello, ladies and gentlemen. First, let me say Merry Christmas to everyone. Tonight has been an incredible night."

Timothy was overwhelmed by the support of not only some of the most important people around Chicago, but by his staff who showed up to assist as well as guests from out of state who were there to sign the papers to take children home with them. There were politicians who showed up with checks and volunteered their time to serve at the buffet table. Musicians who were at the top of the charts that were born and raised in Chicago came back to support the event. The kids danced and sang along with the popular artists, not having a care in the world.

"We started this day with twenty-two children who have been looking for families who would take them in, adopt them, love them and treat them as if they were their own. I'm happy to report that as of this moment, each child we brought here today has been matched with a family and if you all would look around the room, you would see nothing but smiles on the faces of each of those children. This is how it should be," Timothy said.

He was overwhelmed by the pouring out of support he and Holly received in helping the children. When they started down this path, he didn't want even one of them to go a lifetime and never feel the love of parents like he did. He knew how that felt and he didn't want another child to experience that.

Even though he was able to help Holly secure a new property for the children's home, he was hoping, like Holly, that the place would remain empty. It would be funded no matter what and he hoped that each and every child who would come through those doors would immediately find a family to love and cherish them.

"To my staff, thank you for all of the years of dedicated service, not just to me and the company, but to the many people we service each year by going over and above looking for the perfect houses for them. Please check the tree for envelopes with each of your names on them and Merry."

He smiled as he saw a mad rush for the tree by his staff. Everyone else in the room laughed knowing the envelopes most likely contained Christmas bonuses. Christmas wasn't just for the children.

"Now, for my final holiday wish, I want to share that the past month has opened my eyes to so many things that I had been blind to in the past. I realized that the things that kept me from being happy all these years are the things that have now brought me the most joy. Most of you know that I was raised in a group home like the kids who are here today. With the vision of the woman who has stolen my heart, miracles were made here today. I'm glad that what I thought was an endless road of misery, can actually turn out to be the greatest opportunity for happiness. I look around at every child in this room today and every one of them now has a family who will love and cherish them and make sure that they never spend another holiday without a family to call their own. I've spent a lot of years without a family to call my own and now because of Holly, I consider each one of those children as my family because family is everything whether it was yours from birth or acquired over your lifetime."

Timothy searched the room to be sure his eyes were connecting with Holly's as he said his next words. When he saw where she was, he signaled with his eyes to Ariana who walked over to stand next to Holly per his instructions. Jeffrey also moved into place right behind Ariana. Timothy's heart swelled to two times its size knowing what was about to occur.

"I'm hoping to change one aspect of my life tonight to hopefully guarantee that my life is filled with love for a lifetime. Holly, you came into my life and from that first smile, you had me. I have never been as happy as I have been in this last month since we've met and for anyone who never believed in love at first sight, all they need to do is look at the love you and I share and have shared from that first day. You were brought into my life for a reason. It also didn't escape me that I was the biggest bah humbug around and the woman whom I would meet and fall in love with would have a name like Holly Day. That, sweetheart, was no coincidence," he said.

Timothy watched as tears formed in her eyes. He knew she was feeling just as he was. If anyone understood him and what his heart felt, it was her.

"Tonight, I want to make this night extra special. Now that we have made holiday wishes come true for so many families and children, I'm hoping that you will make my one wish come true also. Holly Day, I love you more than any words can say and I hope you will do me the honor of agreeing to be my wife. I love you today, tomorrow and forever," he said as Ariana presented Holly with a ring box.

Holly's world was spinning. Nothing could have prepared her for the words Timothy spoke when he asked her to be his wife. She looked from him and then down at the box red velvet box in the palm of Ariana's hand. With shaky hands and through tears that pooled in her eyes, she took the box from Ariana and opened it. By the time she looked up, Timothy was standing directly in front of her and everyone else in the room had stood and encircled them. She could hear others sniffling at the powerful moment.

"So, what do you say? Do you believe that our coming together was more than just fate, but in fact was destiny?" he asked.

"Yes, I do. I believe in destiny and I believe that's exactly what has happened to us. I love you too and I would marry you today, tomorrow and forever more," Holly said going into his arms.

Everyone around the room cheered for them, especially those who knew the two of them well, knowing what it took for them to get to this day. Timothy held her tight and out of the corner of his eye, he could see her best friend Teresa and her family and his best friend, Kenneth, his wife Cynthia and their kids. He wanted to be sure those that loved the two of them were there for the day that he would make them all one great big family.

"Let's get this ring on your finger right now to make this official," he said.

Holly stepped back from his arms and put her hand out so that he could slip the ring on it. Holly smiled brightly and as soon as he had done so, she went right back into his arms, wrapping them tightly around his neck.

"I love you," she whispered in his ear.

"Baby, I have one more surprise for you," he admitted.

Holly looked at him with confusion and anticipation.

"It was because of you that we were able to bring so many families together with so many children today. I know I said that all of the children had families to now call their own, but that wasn't exactly correct."

Timothy watched as Jeffrey moved from behind Ariana to stand right next to Holly. What Holly had not yet seen was the little girl Jeffrey was holding hands with.

"There was one child whose name didn't make that list. Her name was purposely left off," he said.

He watched as realization set over Holly. She knew he was talking about Angel. It didn't occur to her when she looked at the list earlier that Angel's name had been left off.

She looked down as her hand was joined with an even smaller one. When she turned, she saw Jeffrey was the one who'd placed Angel's hand in hers and the little girl looked up at Holly like she had just saved the little girl's life. The truth was, Holly knew that it was Angel who was not only saving her life, but Timothy's as well. She couldn't speak as tears rolled down her face as Angel lifted her arms up for Holly to pick her up. She didn't hesitate to lift her into her arms, hugging her tightly.

"Holly, tonight our family is already growing. Right after our wedding, Angel is going to come and live with us permanently. I couldn't imagine her being with anyone, but you and me."

Timothy and Holly both looked at Angel as she realized what he'd just said.

Angel jumped happily in Holly's arms.

"Does that mean you and Holly are going to be my mommy and daddy?" she asked looking from Holly to Timothy.

"Yes, Angel. I'm going to be your daddy and Holly is going to be your mommy as soon as we get married," Timothy said.

"When are we getting married?" Angel asked.

Everyone in the room broke out in laughter. Timothy smiled as he tried to explain.

"Well, Holly and I are the ones who are getting married, Angel. Until we are married, you're going to go live with Holly at her house. After that you and Holly can come and live with me at my house. Remember my house?" he asked.

Angel shook her head and her long red ribbon encased braids bounced up and down.

"You have a pool!" she exclaimed.

"Yes, I have a pool. That pool will be yours too, very soon," he said.

"How soon? I want to go swimming," Angel asked.

Timothy didn't have an answer for that. He looked at Holly for help and support with that one.

Holly took over.

"Well, Angel, I think Mr. Timothy and I want to get married as soon as possible, so that we can all live as a family as soon as possible."

She then looked at Timothy.

"Really?" Angel asked.

"What do you say to a New Year's Eve wedding, so that we can start our new year off right? I don't want or need anything big. I just want to be your wife and mother to this little girl here," she said, a little choked up with tears streaming down her face. They were tears of great joy.

"New Year's Eve sounds like a great idea," he agreed.

"I'll help with everything," Ariana chimed in.

"So, will I," other members of his staff added.

"Does this mean I can call you mommy and daddy now? Angel asked.

"Yes, baby girl," Holly said. "You can call us mommy and daddy right now."

"Merry Christmas, everyone!" Angel said.

"Merry Christmas!" the crowd exclaimed around the room as holiday music flooded the air and families stood around the room, each embracing a child who now had a family to call their own.

Timothy and Holly knew their work was just beginning and they were up for the task. They now had their Angel and Timothy could now enjoy every holiday because he now had his Holly Day.

Also available from Cheryl Barton

Bachelor Series:
Bachelor Not For Sale
A Designed Affair
A Perfect Combination

Amorous Occupations Series:
The Artist
The Bookkeeper
The Chef

Upcoming Releases:
Down, But Not Out – December 2013

ABOUT THE AUTHOR

Cheryl Barton lives in Maryland and in her spare time she enjoys reading, writing, spending time with her family, line dancing and eating Maryland steamed crabs.

Visit her website at http://www.cherylbarton.net. You can connect with her on Twitter @mscbarton and on Facebook and Instagram @Author Cheryl Barton.

www.ingramcontent.com/pod-product-compliance
Lightning Source LLC
Chambersburg PA
CBHW050831180626
46814CB00004B/1567